Theodore Watts-Dunton

The Coming of Love

Rhona Boswell's Story, and Other Poems. Fifth Edition

Theodore Watts-Dunton

The Coming of Love
Rhona Boswell's Story, and Other Poems. Fifth Edition

ISBN/EAN: 9783744773201

Printed in Europe, USA, Canada, Australia, Japan

Cover: Foto ©Andreas Hilbeck / pixelio.de

More available books at **www.hansebooks.com**

THE COMING OF LOVE
RHONA BOSWELL'S STORY
AND OTHER POEMS

THE COMING OF LOVE
RHONA BOSWELL'S STORY
AND OTHER POEMS ❧ BY
THEODORE WATTS-DUNTON
AUTHOR OF AYLWIN

JOHN LANE: *The Bodley Head*
LONDON & NEW YORK 1899

FIFTH EDITION

W. H. WHITE AND CO. LTD.
RIVERSIDE PRESS, EDINBURGH

CONTENTS

THE COMING OF LOVE   PAGE

    PERCY BEFORE THE COMING OF LOVE   .   3

    THE DAUGHTER OF THE SUN-RISE .   .   25

CHRISTMAS AT THE MERMAID   .   83

    TALK ON WATERLOO BRIDGE   .   .   149

MISCELLANEOUS POEMS

    A DEAD POET   153

    A GRAVE BY THE SEA   155

    THE OMNIPOTENCE OF LOVE .   .   .   163

    JOHN THE PILGRIM   173

    COLUMBUS   175

b

	PAGE
BEATRICE	177
THE THREE FAUSTS	179
TOAST TO OMAR KHAYYÀM	183
PRAYER TO THE WINDS	187
QUEEN KATHERINE	189
DICKENS RETURNS ON CHRISTMAS DAY	191
THE CHRISTMAS-TREE AT THE PINES	193
PROPHETIC PICTURES AT VENICE	195
WHAT THE SILENT VOICES SAID	209
COLERIDGE	217
CHRISTINA ROSSETTI	219
TO A SLEEPER AT ROME	222
IN A GRAVE-YARD (Oliver Madox-Brown)	224
TWO LETTERS TO A FRIEND	226
ANCESTRAL MEMORY (The deaf and dumb Son of Crœsus)	230
APOLLO IN PARIS	232
AT THE THÉÂTRE FRANÇAIS	238
TO MADAME CARNOT	240

PAGE

THE LAST WALK FROM BOAR'S HILL . 242

THE OCTOPUS OF THE GOLDEN ISLES . 247

LOVE HOLDS OF HEAVEN IN FEE . . 249

THE WOOD-HAUNTER'S DREAM . . 252

MIDSHIPMAN LANYON 254

A REMINISCENCE OF THE OPEN-AIR PLAYS 256

LECONTE DE LISLE 262

TO BRITAIN AND AMERICA (On the death
of Lowell) 265

TO MRS. GARFIELD (On the death of the
President) 267

PREFATORY NOTE TO THE THIRD EDITION

I

A WORD ABOUT RHONA BOSWELL AND SINFI LOVELL

ONE of my most generous critics has said of "The Coming of Love" that, "although published earlier than 'Aylwin,' it is a sequel to the novel." And a sequel it is; so far, at least, as an important character in "Aylwin" is concerned — Rhona Boswell — though between "Aylwin" and "The Coming of Love" another story intervenes.

About Rhona, and about Sinfi Lovell, too, I have received many letters of inquiry—kind letters from entire strangers, which nothing but my late illness, followed by an overwhelming pressure of work in arrear, has prevented me from answering fully and answering most gratefully.

A call for a new edition of "The Coming of Love" gives me an opportunity that I must not let slip of answering these kind friends.

I have said that, so far as regards Rhona Boswell's story, "The Coming of Love" is a sequel to "Aylwin." If the allusions to Rhona's lover, Percy Aylwin, in the prose story have been, in some degree, misunderstood by some readers—if there is any danger of Henry Aylwin, the hero of the novel, being confounded with Percy Aylwin, the hero of this poem—it only shows how difficult it is for the poet or the novelist (who must needs see his characters from the concave side only) to realise that it is the convex side only which he can present to his reader.

The fact is that the motive of "Aylwin"— dealing only as it does with that which is elemental and unchangeable in Man—is of so entirely poetic a nature that I began to write it in verse. After a while, however, I found that a story of so many incidents and complications as the one that was growing under my hand could only be told in prose. This was before I had written any prose at all—yes, it is so long ago as that. And when, afterwards, I began to write criticism, I had (for certain reasons—important then, but of no importance now) abandoned the idea of offering the novel to the outside public at all. Among my friends it had been widely read, both in manuscript and in type.

Now and then I used to draw upon the manuscript for favourite tit-bits of description, etc., to decorate an essay. Certain parts of "The Coming of Love" were written about the same time. The two Aylwins, Henry and Percy, were then very distinct in my own mind; they are very distinct now. And I confess that the possibility of their being confounded with each other had never occurred to me. A certain similarity between the two there must needs be, seeing that the blood of the same Romany ancestress, Fenella Stanley, flows in the veins of both.   I say there must needs be this similarity, because the ancestress was Romany.   For, without starting the inquiry here as to whether or not the Romanies as a race are superior or inferior to all or any of the great European races among which they move, I will venture to affirm that in the Romanies the mysterious energy which the evolutionists call "the prepotency of transmission" in races, is specially strong—so strong, indeed, that evidences of Romany blood in a family may be traced down for several generations.   It is inevitable, therefore, that in each of the descendants of Fenella Stanley, the form taken by the love-passion should show itself in kindred ways.   But the reader who will give a careful study to the characters of Henry and Percy Aylwin, will come to the conclusion, I think, that the similarity between the two is observable in one aspect of their characters only.   The intensity of the love-passion in each assumes a spiritualising and mystical form — akin to nothing so much as to the mystic beauty-worship of Sufism, which teaches that, deeper than Tartarus, stronger than Destiny and Death, the great heart of Nature is beating to the tune of universal love and beauty. But with regard to Romany women, Henry Aylwin's feeling towards them was the very opposite of Percy's. When, in speaking of George Borrow some years ago, I made the remark that between Englishmen of a certain type and gypsy women there is an extraordinary physical attraction—an attraction which did not exist between Borrow and the gypsy women with whom he was brought into contact—I was thinking specially of the character depicted here under the name of Percy Aylwin. And I asked then the question— Supposing Borrow to have been physically drawn with much power towards any woman, could she possibly have been Romany? Would she not rather have been of the Scandinavian type?— would she not have been what he used to call a "Brynhild"? From many conversations with him on this subject, I think she would have been a tall *blonde*, of the type of Isopel Berners—

who, by-the-by, was much more a portrait of a splendid East-Anglian road-girl than is generally imagined. And I think, besides, that Borrow's sympathy with the Anglo-Saxon type may account for the fact that, notwithstanding his love of the free and easy economics of life among the better class of Gryengroes, his gypsy women are all what have been called "scenic characters."

When he comes to delineate a heroine, she is the superb Isopel Berners—that is to say, she is physically (and indeed mentally, too), the very opposite of the Romany *chi*. It was here, as I happen to know, that Borrow's sympathies were with Henry Aylwin far more than with Percy Aylwin.

The type of the Romany *chi*, though very delightful to Henry Aylwin as regards companionship, had no physical attractions for him, otherwise the witchery of the girl here called Rhona Boswell, whom he knew as a child long before Percy Aylwin knew her, must surely have eclipsed such charms as Winifred Wynne or any other winsome

"Gorgie" could possess. On the other hand, it would, I believe, have been impossible for Percy Aylwin to be brought closely and long in contact with a Romany girl like Sinfi Lovell and remain untouched by those unique physical attractions of hers—attractions that made her universally admired by the best judges of female beauty as being the most splendid "face-model" of her time, and as being in form the grandest woman ever seen in the studios—attractions that upon Henry Aylwin seem to have made almost no impression.

There is no accounting for this, as there is no accounting for anything connected with the mysterious witchery of sex. And again, the strong inscrutable way in which some gypsy girls are drawn towards a "Tarno Rye" (as a young English gentleman is called), is quite inexplicable. Some have thought—and Borrow was one of them—that it may arise from that infirmity of the Romany Chal which causes the girls to "take their own part" without appealing to their men-companions for aid — that lack of masculine chivalry among the men of their own race.

II

THE HUMOUR OF THE ROMANY CHI

And now for a word or two upon a matter in connection with "Aylwin" and "The Coming of Love" which interests me more deeply. Some of those who have been specially attracted towards Sinfi Lovell have had misgivings, I find, as to whether she is not an idealisation, an impossible Romany *chi*, and some of those who have been specially attracted towards Rhona Boswell have had the same misgivings as to her.

The *Times*, in a kindly notice of "The Coming of Love," said that the sort of gypsies here depicted are a very interesting people—"unless the author has flattered them unduly."

Those who best know the women of the gypsies will be the first to aver that I have *not* "flattered them unduly."

One of the great racial specialities of the Romany is the superiority of the women to the men.   For it is not merely in intelligence, in imagination, in command over language, in comparative breadth of view regarding the Gorgio world that the Romany women (in Great Britain, at least) leave the men far behind.   In everything that goes to make nobility of character this superiority is equally noticeable.   To imagine a gypsy hero is, I will confess, rather difficult. Not that the average male gypsy is without a certain amount of courage, but it soon gives way, and, in a conflict between a gypsy and an Englishman, it always seems as though ages of oppression have damped the virility of Romany stamina.

Although some of our most notable prize-fighters have been gypsies, it used to be well known, in times when the ring was fashionable, that a gypsy could not always be relied upon to "take punishment" with the stolid indifference of an Englishman or a negro, partly, perhaps, because his more highly-strung nervous system makes him more sensitive to pain.

The courage of a gypsy woman, on the other

hand, has passed into a proverb; nothing seems to daunt it. This superiority of the women to the men extends to everything, unless, perhaps, we except that gift of music for which the gypsies as a race are noticeable. With regard to music, however, even in Eastern Europe (Russia alone excepted), where gypsy music is so universal that, according to some writers, every Hungarian musician is of Romany extraction, it is the men, and not, in general, the women, who excel. Those, however, who knew Sinfi Lovell may think with me that this state of things may simply be the result of opportunity and training.

But it is with regard to the humour of gypsy women that Gorgio readers seem to be most sceptical. The humorous endowment of most races is found to be more abundant and richer in quality among the men than among the women. But among the Romanies the women seem to have taken humour with the rest of the higher qualities.

A question that has been most frequently

asked me in connection with my two gypsy heroines has been—Have gypsy girls really the *esprit* and the humorous charm that you attribute to them? My answer to this question shall be a quotation from Mr Groome's delightful book, "Gypsy Folk-Tales," just published.

Speaking of the Romany *chi's* incomparable piquancy, he says:

"I have known a gypsy girl dash off what was almost a folk-tale impromptu. She had been to a pic-nic in a four-in-hand with 'a lot o' real tip-top gentry'; and 'Reia,' she said to me afterwards, 'I'll tell you the comicalest thing as ever was. We'd pulled up, to put the brake on; and there was a *púro hotchiwitchi* (old hedgehog) come and looked at us through the hedge; looked at me hard. I could see he'd his eye upon me. And home he'd go, that old hedgehog, to his wife, and "Missus," he'd say, "what d'ye think? I seen a little gypsy gal just now in a coach and four horses"; and "*Dábla!*" she'd say, "*sawkúmni 'as vardé kenáw*" ("Bless us! everyone now keeps a carriage ").'"

Now, without saying that this impromptu folk-lorist *was* Rhona Boswell, I will at least aver, without fear of contradiction from Mr Groome, that it might well have been she.

Although there is as great a difference between one Romany *chi* and another, as between one English girl and another, there is a strange and fascinating kinship between the humour of all gypsy girls.

No three girls could possibly be more unlike than Sinfi Lovell, Rhona Boswell, and the girl of whom Mr Groome gives his anecdote; and yet there is a similarity between the fanciful humour of them all.

The humour of Rhona Boswell must speak for itself in these pages—where, however, the passion-ate and tragic side of her character and her story dominates everything. But I cannot resist the temptation of giving an example of Sinfi Lovell's humour, and of her power of dramatic narrative.

It is recorded that years after the events told in "Aylwin," a Gorgio friend of Sinfi Lovell's was crossing Snowdon with her from Capel Curig, and they stopped to observe the same sunrise effects which are described in "Aylwin." The splendours made the friend very voluble, while Sinfi remained silent.   At last he said, "You don't seem to enjoy it a bit, Sinfi."

The slightest of smiles broke over her face as she said, "Don't injiy it, don't I?   *You* injiy talkin' about it.   *I* injiy letting it soak in."

On another occasion the same friend got her to talk about Hurstcote Manor and D'Arcy. He did so with great difficulty, however, for, underlying all her humour, there was, he thought, a sadness bespeaking a heart which, though not broken, was sorely bruised.

"Well," said Sinfi at last, "there ain't much to tell about that.   It's allus a quiet life down there.   Mr D'Arcy's lively enough sometimes; but sometimes he has the blues awful, and lays rollin' on the great brown holland sofy in the

c

studio, a-pickin' his nails an' a-lookin' at nothink. But that ain't so very often; and he is a nice man, an' everybody likes him. There's on'y one 'musin' party down there, an' that's a kind o' housekeeper, a born nataral; they calls her Mrs Titwing."

Sinfi then began to tell the friend some racy anecdotes about D'Arcy's housekeeper, from which it appeared that the painter, after Sinfi had been the means of restoring Winifred Wynne to health, had insisted on the gypsy's being elevated from the position of model to that of a friend and an equal. This had been somewhat resented in the kitchen, and the kind of humorous good sense that was Sinfi's characteristic had enabled her to see that the resentment was but natural under the circumstances.

"You see," said Sinfi, "whenever I went down to Hurstcote Manor before, the sarvents allus used to call me the gypsy model, and you must know that all English Gorgios, whether gentlefolks or sarvents, is allus much more ingorant than the Welsh Gorgios, and they look down on us Romanies in a way as allus makes me laugh."

The Gorgio friend said, in mock reproachfulness: "You forget for the moment your good breeding, Sinfi; I am an English Gorgio."

"I mean Gorgio sarvents, in course," said Sinfi, with ready tact. "It ain't perlite to say Gorgio at all to a Gorgio. Toffs is the word when you're talkin' o' gentlefolk. Howsomedever, what with my dukkurin' an' what with my singin' an' playin' on the crwth, Mr D'Arcy's sarvents used to like to get me in the sarvents' hall, an' used to look forrud to my goin' to Hurstcote. But now, when Mr D'Arcy would keep on treatin' me like a real rawnee, in course it put their noses out o' jint, an' this used to 'muse me. I used to say to the butler, 'That nose o' yourn has got a twist lately, Mr Slater. You don't look quite so straight along it as you used to; what's the matter with it now? Is it 'coz Mr D'Arcy *will* make a rawnee on me? Now, you knows very well,' I sez, 'that I don't want to be made a rawnee on. There ain't a Gorgio lady in the land,' sez I, 'as is fit to hold the candle to a Romany rawnee and a duke's chavi,' I sez. 'The Gorgios is all mumply when set by the side of a Romany.'"

"Lady Sinfi!" the friend exclaimed, in a still more reproachful tone.

"Of course, when I said that," exclaimed Sinfi, "I hadn't seen much of nice, kind Gorgies. Well, this used to make the butler laugh an' seem half ashamed of hisself, an' he used to say, 'It's all right, my gal; us sarvents allus liked you, Sinfi; and though it *is* a bit queer to see you a-settin' down at table with the guvernor and the lady-model, this is Topsy-Turvey Hall, you know; that's what we calls it, an' it's a lark to see you three a-settin' there, an' it makes a little fun in this dull place. At first we did jib at it a bit, but now we're got used to it we like it; but it's that bloomin' Mrs Titwing as has got her back set up about it, an' she's allus a-talkin' to me and the cook an' all of us about the insult to us of Mr D'Arcy's goin's-on; and if it *is* insultin' for you to be a-settin' there, sarvents are very thin-skinned about bein' insulted, you know.'

"That's what he sez. The housekeeper, you must know, is a sort o' stuck-up, gray-eyed, born nataral, as ain't got all her buttons. Afore I got there she used to be allus a-talkin' about the difference atween her as is a lady an' the sarvents, an' about her bein' nearer to the parlour folk than the sarvents' hall. Well, this 'ere born nataral, Mrs Titwing, bein' a Christian rawnee, used to think that the more she hated the heathen gypsies, as she called us, the more she wur a-sayin' her prayers; an' this made her be so friendly all at wonst with the sarvents, an' egg 'em on to set up a kind of a scrimmage agin' me, though they done it in a kind o' half-hearted way, as I see'd. So one day I told Mr D'Arcy about it, and I sez to him, 'Jist to make peace with the born nataral, who's very ingorant and don't know no better, I think I had better have my vittles in the sarvents' hall as I used to; it don't make no difference to me. If a born nataral, as is a mumply Gorgio to boot, looks down on me, *I* looks down on all born natarals, and all Gorgios too—if they're mumply.'

"But Mr D'Arcy jumps off his paintin'-stool and begins to swear an' bawl out, till he makes the room ring agin, an' he sez, 'Pull that 'ere bell, Sinfi,' an' I does, an' in comes one o' the sarvents, an' Mr D'Arcy sez, 'Send that — that Mrs Titwing here, an' then go an' tell all the sarvents to come up ; I wants to speak to 'em.' An' up comes the born nataral, lookin' about the eyes as if she'd jist been a-peelin' ingins. An' when Mr D'Arcy claps eyes on her, he sez, 'A nice kind of a Christian woman you are ! I suppose you think the more you spit in the face of the heathen gypsy, as you call my friend Sinfi, the more you show your love for the Lord Jesus. But look you here, Mrs Titwing, the Lord Jesus, when you get to them Golden Gates o' Heaven as you are very anxious to get thro', He'll say, " What do you want here, Mrs Titwing? It's the other gates across the way as opens for such as you. It ain't *me* as *you* takes arter, Mrs Titwing; it's the gent over the way," and then the porter o' them golden gates he'll jist give you a gentle kick, an' say, " Out you goes, Mrs Titwing, out you goes." An' presto! you'll find yourself behind them other gates as belongs to the other party, where all the congregation of Little Bethel of Hurstcote village is waitin' for you.' And when all the other sarvents comes in, Mr D'Arcy he makes them stand in a row afore him; and then he pints to me and sez, 'You see that Romany *chi*?'

"See what, Sinfi?" asked the friend.

"Well, of course, he didn't say Romany *chi*, he said—'You see Sinfi—suppose that she'd done any one on you a great sarvice, and brought herself to death's door a-doin' on it. Suppose she saved you from bein' burnt in your beds, say, or drownded in the weir, say, should you feel friendly-like towards that gypsy model, or unfriendly?' And they all sez at wonst, 'In course, sir, we should feel friendly-like, and *very* friendly-like.' 'Well,' sez Mr D'Arcy, 'Sinfi Lovell has done *me*, an' a dear friend o' mine, a great sarvice at the risk of her own life, she has. And the doctor tells me that it will do her good to be nussed up in the parlour, an' have her meals along o' me. What should you think of me if I turned round and said, "No, she shan't, because she's a gypsy model"?' Then the parlour-maid what hates the born nataral, sez, 'I should say it wasn't a bit like Mr D'Arcy, but a good deal like a fine Christian lady what shall be nameless; a lady wot sez her prayers reg'lar, an' tries to set people agin each other.' Then they all began to laugh, an' the born nataral began to cry; and there were an end of the row."

But I think enough has here been said to show how richly endowed are the Romany girls with humour.

III

CHRISTMAS AT THE MERMAID

Since the appearance of this volume, there has been a great deal of acute and learned discussion as to the identity of that mysterious "friend" of Shakspeare, to whom so many of the sonnets are addressed. But everything that has been said upon the subject seems to fortify me in the opinion that "no critic has been able to identify" that friend. Southampton seems at first to fit into the sacred place; so does Pembroke at first. But, after a while, true and unbiassed criticism rejects them both. I therefore feel more than ever justified in "imagining the friend for myself." And this, at least, I know, that to have been the friend of Shakspeare, a man must needs have been a lover of nature;—he must have been a lover of England, too. And upon these two points, and upon another—the movement of a soul dominated by friendship as a passion—I have tried to show Shakspeare's probable influence upon his "friend of friends." It would have been a mistake, however, to cast the sonnets in the same metrical mould as Shakspeare's.

T. W.-D.

Christmas 1898.

PREFATORY NOTE TO FIRST AND SECOND EDITIONS

HAD it not been for the intervention of matters of a peculiarly absorbing kind — matters which caused me to delay the task of collecting these verses—I should have been the most favoured man who ever brought out a volume of poems, for they would have been printed by William Morris, at the Kelmscott Press. As that projected edition of his was largely subscribed for, a word of explanation to the subscribers is, I am told, required from me. Among the friends who saw much of that great poet and beloved man during the last year of his life, there was one who would not and could not believe that he would die—myself. To me he seemed human vitality concentrated to a point of quenchless light; and when the appalling truth that he must dic did at last strike through me, I had no heart and no patience to think about anything in connection with him but the loss that was to come upon us. And, now, whatsoever pleasure I may feel at seeing my verses in one of Mr Lane's inviting little volumes will be dimmed and marred by the thought that Morris's name also might have been, and is not, on the imprint.

With regard to the two chief poems in the volume, perhaps I ought to offer an explanatory word or two. The gypsies depicted in "The Coming of Love" belong to a peculiar class, the East Anglian and East Midland horse-dealers from Wales. At horse fairs no dealers are so clever as they in seeing the points of a horse, buying him at the lowest price possible, and selling him at the highest. Hence they are often as prosperous as the mongrel vagabonds and London tramps, classed as "gypsies" by such writers as the late well-intentioned George Smith of Coalville, are squalid.

With regard to "Christmas at the Mermaid," such liberties as I may, here and there, have taken with the history of the Jacobean period, are not such, I hope, as will vex the student. And as concerns the mysterious friend of Shakspeare, to whom so many of his sonnets were addressed, I consider that no critic has been able to identify him, and that I am entitled to imagine that friend for myself.

T. W.-D.

THE COMING OF LOVE

RHONA BOSWELL'S STORY

CHARACTERS

PERCY AYLWIN of Rington Manor, Kinsman of HENRY AYLWIN of Raxton Hall.

RHONA BOSWELL, nicknamed "Merrylaugh the Rider."

THE COMING OF LOVE

RHONA BOSWELL'S STORY

Part I

PERCY BEFORE THE COMING OF LOVE

A

.

THE COMING OF LOVE

RHONA BOSWELL'S STORY

Part I

PERCY BEFORE THE COMING OF LOVE

I

A STARRY NIGHT AT SEA

If heaven's bright halls are very far from sea,

I dread a pang the angels could not 'suage:

The imprisoned seabird knows, and only he,

How drear, how dark, may be the proudest

    cage.

Outside the bars he sees a prison still:

The self-same wood or mead or silver stream

That lends the captive lark a joyous thrill

Is landscape in the seabird's prison-dream.

So might I pine on yonder starry floor

For sea-wind, deaf to all the singing spheres;

Billows like these, that never knew a shore,

Might mock mine eyes and tease my hungry

    ears ;

No scent of amaranth, moly, or asphodel,

In lands that bloom above yon glittering

    vault,

Could soothe me if I lost this briny smell,

This living breath of Ocean, sharp and salt.

II

NATURE'S FOUNTAIN OF YOUTH

(A morning swim off Guernsey with a Friend.)

As if the Spring's fresh groves should change

    and shake

To dark green woods of Orient terebinth,

Then break to bloom of England's hyacinth,

So 'neath us change the waves, rising to take

Each kiss of colour from each cloud and flake

Round many a rocky hall and labyrinth,

Where sea-wrought column, arch, and granite
     plinth,

Show how the sea's fine rage dares make and
     break.

Young with the youth the sea's embrace can
     lend,

Our glowing limbs, with sun and brine
     empearled,

Seem born anew, and in your eyes, dear friend,

Rare pictures shine, like fairy flags unfurled,

Of child-land, where the roofs of rainbows
     bend

Over the magic wonders of the world.

III

THE LANGUAGE OF NATURE'S FRAGRANCY

(The Tiring-room in the Rocks.)

THESE are the " Coloured Caves " the sea-maid
    built ;
Her walls are stained beyond that lonely fern,
For she must fly at every tide's return,
And all her sea-tints round the walls are
    spilt.
Outside behold the bay, each headland gilt
With morning's gold ; far off the foam-
    wreaths burn
Like fiery snakes, while here the sweet waves
    yearn
Up sand more soft than Avon's sacred silt.
And smell the sea ! no breath of wood or
    field,
From lips of may or rose or eglantine,

Comes with the language of a breath benign,

Shuts the dark room where glimmers Fate
revealed,

Calms the vext spirit, balms a sorrow
unhealed,

Like scent of seaweed rich of morn and brine.

IV

LOVE BRINGS WARNING OF NATURA MALIGNA

(PERCY *sailing with a friend past the Casket Lighthouse.*)

AMID the Channel's wiles and deep decoys,

Where yonder Beacons watch the siren-sea,

A girl was reared who knew nor flower nor
tree

Nor breath of grass at dawn, yet had high
joys:

The moving lawns whose verdure never cloys
Were hers.   At last she sailed to Alderney,
But there she pined.   "The bustling world,"
    said she,
" Is all too full of trouble, full of noise."
The storm-child, fainting for her home, the
    storm,
Had winds for sponsor—one proud rock for
    nurse,
Whose granite arms, through countless years,
    disperse
All billowy squadrons tide and wind can form :
The cold bright sea was hers for universe
Till o'er the waves Love flew and fanned them
    warm.

But Love brings Fear with eyes of augury :—
Her lover's boat was out; her ears were
    dinned

With sea-sobs warning of the awakened wind

That shook the troubled sun's red canopy.

Even while she prayed the storm's high revelry

Woke petrel, gull — all revellers winged and
    finned—

And clutched a sail brown-patched and weather-
    thinned,

And then a swimmer fought a white, wild sea.

"My songs are louder, child, than prayers of
    thine,"

The Mother sang. "Thy sea-boy waged no strife

With Hatred's poison, gangrened Envy's
    knife—

With me he strove, in deadly sport divine,

Who lend to men, to gods, an hour of life,

Then give them sleep within these arms of
    mine!"

V

MOTHER CAREY'S CHICKEN

(PERCY, *on seeing a storm-petrel in a cage on a cottage wall near Gypsy Dell, takes down the cage with the view of releasing the bird.*)

I CANNOT brook thy gaze, belovèd bird;
  That sorrow is more than human in thine
    eye;
Too deeply, brother, is my spirit stirred
  To see thee here, beneath the landsmen's
    sky,
Cooped in a cage with food thou canst not
    eat,
Thy "snow-flake" soiled, and soiled those
    conquering feet
That walked the billows, while thy "*sweet-
    sweet-sweet*"
      Proclaimed the tempest nigh.

Bird whom I welcomed while the sailors cursed,

   Friend whom I blessed wherever keels may

      roam,

Prince of my childish dreams, whom mermaids

      nursed

   In purple of billows—silver of ocean-foam,

Abashed I stand before the mighty grief

That quells all other: Sorrow's King and

      Chief,

Who rides the wind and holds the sea in fief,

      Then finds a cage for home!

From out thy jail thou seest yon heath and

      woods,

   But canst thou hear the birds or smell the

      flowers?

Ah, no! those rain-drops twinkling on the

      buds

   Bring only visions of the salt sea-showers.

"The sea!" the linnets pipe from hedge and
    heath ;
"The sea!" the honeysuckles whisper and
    breathe,
And tumbling waves, where those wild-roses
    wreathe,
      Murmur from inland bowers.

These winds so soft to others—how they burn !
  The mavis sings with gurgle and ripple and
    plash,
To thee yon swallow seems a wheeling tern ;
    And when the rain recalls the briny lash,
Old Ocean's kiss we love—oh, when thy sight
Is mocked with Ocean's horses—manes of
    white,
The long and shadowy flanks, the shoulders
    bright—
      Bright as the lightning's flash—

When all these scents of heather and brier and
    whin,
  All kindly breaths of land-shrub, flower, and
    vine,
Recall the sea-scents, till thy feathered skin
  Tingles in answer to a dream of brine—
When thou, remembering there thy royal
    birth,
Dost see between the bars a world of dearth,
Is there a grief—a grief on all the earth—
    So heavy and dark as thine ?

But I can buy thy freedom—I (thank God !),
  Who loved thee more than albatross or
    gull—
Loved thee, and loved the waves thy footsteps
    trod—
  Dreamed of thee when, becalmed, we lay
    a-hull—

'Tis I, thy friend, who once, a child of six,

To find where Mother Carey fed her chicks,

Climbed up the boat and then with bramble
    sticks

      Tried all in vain to scull—

Thy friend who shared thy Paradise of Storm—

    The little dreamer of the cliffs and coves,

Who knew thy mother, saw her shadowy
    form

    Behind the cloudy bastions where she
    moves,

And heard her call: "Come! for the welkin
    thickens,

And tempests mutter and the lightning
    quickens!"

Then, starting from his dream, would find the
    chickens

      Were daws or blue rock-doves—

Thy friend who owned another Paradise,

    Of calmer air, a floating isle of fruit,

Where sang the Nereids on a breeze of spice,

    While Triton, from afar, would sound

        salute :

There wast thou winging, though the skies

        were calm ;

For marvellous strains, as of the morning's

        shalm,

Were struck by ripples round that isle of

        palm

        Whose shores were Ocean's lute.

And now to see thee here, my king, my king,

    Far-glittering memories mirrored in those

        eyes,

As if there shone within each iris-ring

    An orbèd world — ocean and hills and

        skies !—

Those black wings ruffled whose triumphant
    sweep
Conquered in sport !—yea, up the glimmering
    steep
Of highest billow, down the deepest deep,
    Sported with victories !—

To see thee here !—a coil of wilted weeds
    Beneath those feet that danced on diamond
    spray,
Rider of sportive Ocean's reinless steeds—
    Winner in Mother Carey's Sabbath-fray
When, stung by magic of the Witch's
    chant,
    They rise, each foamy-crested combatant—
They rise and fall and leap and foam and gallop
    and pant
    Till albatross, sea-swallow, and cormorant
    Must flee like doves away !

And shalt thou ride no more where thou hast
  ridden,
    And feast no more in hyaline halls and
    caves,
Master of Mother Carey's secrets hidden,
    Master and monarch of the wind and waves,
Who never, save in stress of angriest blast,
Asked ship for shelter—never till at last
The foam-flakes hurled against the sloping
    mast
        Slashed thee like whirling glaives ?

Right home to fields no seamew ever kenned,
    Where scarce the great sea-wanderer fares
    with thee,
I come to take thee—nay, 'tis I, thy friend !
    Ah, tremble not—I come to set thee free ;
I come to tear this cage from off this wall,
And take thee hence to that fierce festival

B

Where billows march and winds are musical,

Hymning the Victor-Sea !

      *   *   *   *   *

Yea, lift thine eyes to mine. Dost know me

now ?

Thou'rt free ! thou'rt free ! Ah, surely a

bird can smile !

Dost know me, Petrel ? Dost remember how

I fed thee in the wake for many a mile,

Whilst thou wouldst pat the waves, then,

rising, take

The morsel up and wheel about the wake ?

Thou'rt free, thou'rt free, but for thine own

dear sake

I keep thee caged awhile.

Away to sea ! no matter where the coast :

The road that turns for home turns never

wrong ;

Where waves run high my bird will not be

    lost :

His home I know : 'tis where the winds are

    strong—

Where, on a throne of billows, rolling hoary

And green and blue and splashed with sunny

    glory,

Far, far from shore—from farthest promon-

    tory—

Prophetic Nature bares the secret of the story

    That holds the spheres in song !

(PERCY, *carrying the bird in the cage, turns to cross
a rustic wooden bridge leading past Gypsy Dell, when
he suddenly comes upon a landsman-friend of his, a
"Scholar-Gypsy," who is just parting from a young
Gypsy-girl, dressed in the picturesque costume of the
well-to-do "Gryengroes," or horse-dealers. She is
carrying in one hand a fishing-rod, and in the other
an osier-wythe, upon which three or four fish are
strung by the gills. With the evening sun falling
upon her lustrous eyes and illuminating the rich
colour of her face, the girl presents a picture of
such striking beauty that* PERCY *stands dazzled*

and forgets the petrel. The bird pushes its way through the half-open door and flies away. As the two friends stand and watch the Gypsy-girl passing down the Dell, the Scholar-Gypsy relates many anecdotes of her—anecdotes which teach PERCY *that the land is richer than the sea, and teach him also that, through the unsophisticated movements of the female heart, Natura Benigna can express herself.)*

VI

NATURA BENIGNA REVEALED THROUGH A GYPSY-CHILD

The Scholar-Gypsy's story of Rhona Boswell as a Child

"THE child arose and danced through frozen
   dells,

Drawn by the Christmas chimes, and soon she
   sate

Where, 'neath the snow around the churchyard
   gate,

The ploughmen slept in bramble-banded cells:

Gentiles.   The gorgios pass'd, half-fearing gypsy-spells,

While Rhona gazing seem'd to meditate ;

Then laugh'd for joy, then wept disconsolate :

' De poor dead gorgios cannot hear de bells.'

Within the church the clouds of gorgio-breath

Arose, a steam of lazy praise and prayer

To Him who weaves the loving Christmas-
　　stair

O'er sorrow and sin and wintry deeps of Death ;

But where stood He ? Beside our Rhona
　　there,

Remembering childish tears in Nazareth." *

* For this anecdote of Rhona Boswell as a child I am
indebted to my friend Francis Hindes Groome, author of
" In Gipsy Tents " and the Romany novel, " Kriegspiel,"

CONCLUSION OF PART I

THE COMING OF LOVE

RHONA BOSWELL'S STORY

Part II

THE DAUGHTER OF THE SUNRISE

THE COMING OF LOVE

RHONA BOSWELL'S STORY

PART II

THE DAUGHTER OF THE SUNRISE

RHONA'S FIRST KISS

(PERCY *alone in Rington Furze :* RHONA *has just left him.*)

IF only in dreams may Man be fully blest,

Is heaven a dream ?   Is she I claspt a dream ?

Or stood she here even now where dew-drops

    gleam

And miles of furze shine yellow down the

    West?

I seem to clasp her still—still on my breast

Her bosom beats : I see the bright eyes beam.

I think she kiss'd these lips, for now they seem

Scarce mine: so hallow'd of the lips they
    press'd.
Yon thicket's breath——can that be eglantine?
Those birds——can they be Morning's choristers?
Can this be Earth? Can these be banks of
    furze?
Like burning bushes fired of God they shine!
I seem to know them, though this body of mine
Passed into spirit at the touch of hers!

II

THE GOLDEN HAND *

PERCY.

Do you forget that day on Rington strand
When, near the crumbling ruin's parapet,

   * Among the Gypsies of all countries the happiest pos-
sible "Dukkeripen" (*i.e.*, prophetic symbol of Natura
Mystica) is a hand-shaped golden cloud floating on the sky.
It is singular that the same idea is found among races

I saw you stand beside the long-shore net

The gorgios spread to dry on sun-lit sand?

RHONA.

Do I forget?

PERCY.

You wove the wood-flowers in a dewy band

Around your hair which shone as black as

    jet:

No fairy's crown of bloom was ever set

Round brows so sweet as those the wood-

    flowers spanned.

I see that picture now; hair dewy-wet:

Dark eyes that pictures in the sky expand:

entirely disconnected with them—the Finns, for instance,
with whom Ukko, the "sky god" or "angel of the sunrise," was called the "golden king" and "leader of the
clouds," and his Golden Hand was more powerful than
all the army of Death. The "Golden Hand" is sometimes called the Lover's Dukkeripen.

Good-luck. Love-lips (with one tattoo "for dukkerin")
tanned

By sunny winds that kiss them as you stand.

RHONA.

Do I forget?

The Golden Hand shone there: it's *you* forget,

Or p'raps us Romanies ondly understand

The way the Lovers' Dukkeripen is planned

Which shone that second time when us two met.

PERCY.

Blest "Golden Hand"!

RHONA.

The wind, that mixed the smell o' violet

Wi' chirp o' bird, a-blowin' from the land

Where my dear mammy lies, said as it fanned

My heart-like, "Them 'ere tears makes mammy
fret."

She loves to see her chavi lookin' grand,   Child.

So I made what you call'd a coronet,

And in the front I put her amulet :

She sent the Hand to show she sees me yet.

PERCY.

Blest " Golden Hand " !

III

RHONA'S LOVE LETTER AFTER PERCY'S
FIRST STAY IN GYPSY DELL

Gypsy Dell, Wensdy.

THIS ere comes hoppen, leaven me the same,

And lykwise all our breed in Gypsy Dell,

Barrin the spotted gry, wot's turned up lame ;   Horse.

A crick have made his orfside fetlock swell.

The Scollard's larnen me to rite and spel,

It's 'ard, but then I longed to rite your name :

Them squrruls in the Dell have grow'd that
  tame!
  How sweet the haycocks smel!

Faith. Dordi! how I should like you just to see
The Scollard when he's larnen me to rite,
A buzzin like a chafer or a bee,
Eyes. Else cussen you wi' bloodshot yockers bright
Mouth,
teeth. And moey girnin, danniers gleamin white.
He's wuss nor ever follerin arter me,
Peepin roun' every bush an every tree
  Mornin and noon and night.

When I wur standin by the river's brim,
Birds. Hearin the chirikels in Rington wood,
And seein the moorhens larn their chicks to
  swim,
Thinks I, "I hears the Scollard's heavy
  thud";

And when I turned, behold ye, there he stood!

He says I promised as I'd marry him,

And if I di'n't he'd tear me limb from limb.

    Sez I, " That's if you could."

But when I thinks o' you, a choon aglall,   A month ago.

Dray mendys tan a-studyin Romany—   In our tent.

Nock, danniers, moey, yockers, canners, bal—   Nose, teeth, mouth, eyes, ears, hair.

It make me sometime larf and sometime cry ;

And that make Granny's crinkles crinkle sly ;

" Dabla !" my daddy says, " de* blesséd gal   Faith.

Shall lel herself a tarnow Rye she shall—   Get. Young gentleman. Gypsy gentleman.

    A tarnow Romany Rye."

I lets em larf, but well I knows—too well—

The ondly tarnow Rye, and ondly man,

That in my dreams I sometime seem to lel   Get.

Ain't for the lyks o' mee in this 'ere tan,   Tent.

---

* The gypsies of the present generation cease, except in childhood, to say " de" for " the."

The Rye wot sat by mee where Dell-brook
    ran,
And larnt my Romany words and used to tell
Sich sweet, strange things all day, till shadders
    fell
       And light o' stars began.

Mose nights I lays awake, but when the cock
Begin to crow and rooks begin to fly
And chimes come livelier out o' Rington clock,
It's then I sees your pictur in the sky
(So plane, it seems to bring the mornin' nigh),
Hair, teeth, Bal, danniers, canners, yockers, moey, nock :
ears, eyes,
mouth, nose. My daddy's bort me sich a nicet new frock.

Your loving   Your comly korly chy.
dark girl.

IV

PERCY READING THE LETTER AT RINGTON MANOR

THE trees awake: I hear the branches creak!

And ivy-leaves are tapping at the pane:

Dawn draws across the grey a saffron streak,

To let me read at sunrise once again

Beautiful Rhona's letter, which has lain,

Balming the pillow underneath my cheek,

While in the dark her writing seemed to speak:

　　　Her great eyes lit my brain.

I felt the paper—felt her thumb's device

That stamped the wax; I seemed to feel the
　　　fingers

Which wrote these misspelt words of rarer price

Than songs of bards I worshipped as the
　　　bringers

C

Of light from shores where spheral music
    lingers,
Till came this girl, whose music could entice
My soul to that diviner Paradise
    Where lovers are the singers—

That Paradise which Rhona can transfer
From Eden to the tents of Gypsy Dell,
Where Love is still his own orthographer
As when on scriptured leaves of asphodel
He taught his earliest pupil, Eve, to spell—
Where Love speaks out what makes his bosom
    stir
Frankly as yonder woodland chorister,
    Whose first notes rise and swell.

V

EVENING ON THE RIVER

PERCY AND RHONA.

MORE mellow falls the light and still more
    mellow

Around the boat, as we two glide along

'Tween grassy banks she loves where, tall and
    strong,

The buttercups stand gleaming, smiling, yellow.

She knows the nightingales of " Portobello ; "

Love makes her know each bird ! In all that
    throng

No voice seems like another : soul is song,

And never nightingale was like its fellow ;

For, whether born in breast of Love's own bird,

Singing its passion in those islet-bowers

Whose sunset-coloured maze of leaves and
    flowers

The rosy river's glowing arms engird,

Or born in human souls—twin souls like

ours—

Song leaps from deeps unplumbed by spoken

word.

VI

THE NATURE WORSHIPPER AND WOMAN'S
WITCHERY

(PERCY *walking along the river-side near Gypsy Dell
at break of day.*)

LOVE knows a wrong no tears can ever atone:

A word can break the web of Passion's spell,

And then away the enchanted woof is blown

That made a faery world of wood and dell:

But direr than all direst words are deeds :—

Can I, who saw her body shake and sway

Before a storm of rage, like yonder reeds

When March winds bend them o'er the water-
  weeds—

Can I forgive that wrong of yesterday ?—

Can I, who saw the lips of this wild girl,

So loving once, shrink back till pearly teeth,

That once seemed lovelier than the morning's
  pearl,

Flashed bright as that bright blade she dared
  unsheathe—

Can I, who saw a brow, a throbbing throat

Glassed in the stream beneath the willow tree,

As up she sprang, a tigress, in the boat—

Can I forgive her, though the siren wrote

The loveliest letter in the world to me ?

> (*He comes upon a second letter from* RHONA *lying on the
> grass, and stands looking at it with yearning eyes, but
> afraid to pick it up.*)

Another letter !   Ah, full well I know

Those characters so childish, big, and round:

I think she watches where the hawthorns throw

Those shortening shadows on the dewy ground.

Ah yes! that head which gleams by yonder
bush,

Where golden shafts from out the quiver of
morn

Pierce the wet leaves and wake the hidden
thrush—

That cheek which seems to lend a lovelier blush

To blushing may-buds on the dew-bright thorn!

(He takes up the letter and reads it aloud.)

THE LETTER.

This time you can't forgive me—*that* I know—

But when I'm dead o' cryin and in the groun,

You'll come, afore my grass has time to grow,

And say, " That's hern ; the clods is fresh and
brown.

Lord, how I misses her in puv and tan,"

Field.
Tent.

You'll say, "that gal wot axed me to forgive
  her !
It druv her mad to see me kis my han
And smile so sweet — pore Rhona's ondly
  man !—
To that fine rawni rowin on the river.   Lady.

Pore gal," you'll say, " she never touched her
  knife,
Leaseways, just touched the handel so," you'll
  say ;
" She'd never ha' drawed : she wur to bee my
  wife,
And loved me, loved me, loved me night and
  day.
What made the chi," you'll say, " start from the Girl.
  seat ?
What made her flesh goo hot and cold and
  shiver

Right down her back-like—yis, from hed to
  feet ?
She seed me kis my han and smile so swete
To that fine rawni rowin on the river.

The Dell," you'll say, "do seem that dul and
  sad ;
It dreems o' one wot loved me body and soul,
And loved me most that day I druv her madd

Poor heart. And turned her choori zee to burnin coal ;

Birds. The   The chiriklos 'ull chirp ' He should ha' gien
birds attend
the funeral
of a true   All them sweet smiles—yis, all he had to give
Romany
maid.   her—
To her we buried with her Romany kin,
And laid wi' clods all round her eyes an' chin,
Through that fine rawni rowin on the river.'"

You'll say, "Instead o' havin Jasper's gal,
So spry at snare and rod and landin net,

This teeny clisson from her korley bal

Is all, and that'll ondly make me frett.

I'd sooner fish wi' her where swallows fan

The brook," you'll say, "where water creases

    quiver,

Tryin to hide the trouts, but never can,

Than smile so sweet and look and kis my han

To that fine rawni rowin on the river.

Lock from
her dark
hair. Clisson
really means
a lock for a
key.

"Twur here," you'll say, "where many and

    many a night

We stayed a-settin snares in Gypsy Dell

Beneath the stars, or when the moon wur

    bright,

Till 'twitter' came the arliest chirikel,

And larks the sunshine turned to specks o' gold

Flew whistlin up, but none as could deliver

A tale o' love like that as then wur told

By that pore Rhona, her wot's dead and cold."

Bird.

PERCY.

The witching rogue !   But still I can't forgive
her.

THE LETTER CONTINUED.

Two months
ago.
    " 'Twur here," you'll say, " 'twur here, dooey
       choons aglal,

Tent.
    Out o' her daddy's tan one night there crep'

Handsome.
    A gal to meet me—sich a rinkeni gal—

    Though well she knowed the watch the Scol-
       lard kep' :

    She stayed wi' me till all the eastern sky

    Biled, steamed, and broke to many a fiery slivver

Field and
tent and
sleeping
horse.
    That lit up puv and tan and sooterin grei " :

    You'll seem to feel her lips—

RHONA.

(*Advancing from the bush, watching him as he reads,
then rushing towards him, covering his eyes with her
hands, and pulling down his head and kissing him.*)

       These lips, my Rye !

PERCY.

These lips, indeed ! Ah ! who would not for-

give her ?

RHONA.

Lips as 'ud turn to clods without you, dear !

PERCY.

But how this loving Rhona tries my love !

RHONA.

And yet she'd walk the world barefoot to hear

Them words o' yourn in tan or vesh or puv— Tent, wood, field.

Yis, walk and never know her feet wur sore

To hear you say, " Ah ! who would not forgive

her ? "

PERCY.

But that young lady ?

RHONA.

Her what flicks her oar ?

PERCY.

The same.

RHONA.

You'll never kiss your han no more

To that fine rawni rowin on the river?

VII

OCEAN-SORCERY

*(PERCY on the deck of " The Petrel " after he has
been separated from RHONA.)*

WAS it indeed but two sweet years ago

When once a sailor on a star-lit sea

Babbled about its spell, and did not know

How Love makes Nature breathe her poesy?

When did the sea-spell vanish? On that day

When his beloved petrel flew away.

But as for them who bade him, made him, come,

Though love had crowned him man, to thee,
    wild Ocean,

Prated of some nepenthe in thy foam

To quell his love as by a magic potion—

Some anodyne within thy billowy swirl

To soothe the body—make the soul forget

Its guileless passion for a " guileful girl "

Whose beauty caught him in a " Gypsy
    net "—

They should be here to see these billows
    heaving

Beneath yon Southern Cross that holds the
    sky,

They should be here to see how thou art
    weaving

Pictures of home by ocean-sorcery !

A dingle's fragrance breathed from every
    billow,

Sweeter than Orient frankincense and myrrh—

A slim girl-angler shown beneath a willow,

Leaning against its mossy bole for pillow,

Must needs recall his every thought to her!

VIII

THE MUSIC OF NATURA MYSTICA

(PERCY *on board "The Petrel" in the Pacific,
cruising among coral islands.*)

LAST Sunday morn I thought this azure isle

Was dreaming mine own dream; each bower

    of balm

That spiced the rich Pacific, every palm,

Smiled with the dream that lends my life its

    smile.

" These waves," I said, " lapping the coral pile

Make music like a well-remembered psalm :

Surely an English Sunday, breathing calm,

Broods in each tropic dell, each flowery aisle."

The heav'ns were dreaming, too, of English
skies:

Upon the blue, within a belt of grey,

A well-known spire was pictured far away;

And then I heard a psalm begin to rise,

And saw a dingle—smelt its new-mown hay

Where we two loitered—loitered lover-wise.

IX

LOVE'S CALENTURE

(PERCY *on board* "*The Petrel*" *in a tropic calm.*)

I HEAR our blackbirds singing in our grove,

And now I see—I smell—the eglantine—

The meadow-sweet where rivulets laugh and
shine

To English clouds that laugh and shine above;

I feel a stream of maiden-music move,

Pouring through all my frame a life divine

From Rhona's throbbing bosom claspt to

    mine—

From that dear harp, her heart, whose chords

    are love!

Vanished!—

        O God! a blazing world of sea—

A blistered deck—an engine's grinding jar—

Hot scents of scorching oil and paint and tar—

And, in the offing up yon fiery lee,

One spot in the air no bigger than a bee—

A frigate-bird that sails alone afar!

(He takes from his pocket and reads a letter from RHONA
which reached him in Australia.)

THE LETTER.

On Christmas-eve I seed in dreams the day

When Herne the Scollard comed and said to

    me,

" He's off, that rye o' yourn, gone clean away   Gentleman.

Till swallow-time; he's left this letter: see."

In dreams I heerd the bee and grasshopper,

Like on that mornin, buz in Rington Hollow,

"She'll live till swallow-time and then she'll

     mer,   Die.

For never will a rye come back to her   Gentleman.

Wot leaves her till the comin o' the swallow."

All night I heerd them bees and grasshoppers;

All night I smelt the breath o' grass and may,

Mixed sweet wi' smells o' honey from the

     furze,

Like on that mornin' when you went away;

All night I heerd in dreams my daddy sal   Laugh.

Sayin, " De blessed chi ud give de chollo   Girl, Whole.

O' Bozzle's breed—tans, vardey, greis, and all—   Tents, waggons, horses.

To see dat tarno rye o' hern palall   Back.

Wot's left her till the comin o' the swallow."

I woke and went a-walkin on the ice

All white with snow-dust, just like sparklin

Salt.   loon,

And soon beneath the stars I heerd a v'ice,

Hear.   A v'ice I knowed and often, often shoon;

Smoke.   And then I seed a shape as thin as tuv;

Spirit.   I knowed it wur my blessed mammy's mollo.*

"Rhona," she sez, "that tarno rye you love,

Weep.   He's thinkin on you; don't you go and rove;

You'll see him at the comin o' the swallow."

Sez she, "For you it seemed to kill the grass

When he wur gone, and freeze the brooklets'

Songs.   gillies;

Hay.   There worn't no smell, dear, in the sweetest cas,

And when the summer brought the water-lilies,

Wheat.   And when the sweet winds waved the golden giv,

---

* Mostly pronounced "mullo," but sometimes in the East Midlands "mollo."

The skies above 'em seemed as bleak and
    kollo *   Black.

As now, when all the world seems frozen yiv. Snow.

The months are long, but mammy says you'll
    live

By thinkin o' the comin o' the swallow."

She sez, "The whinchat soon wi' silver throat

Will meet the stonechat in the buddin whin,

And soon the blackcap's airliest gillic 'ull float Song.

From light-green boughs through leaves a-peepin
    thin ;

The wheat-ear soon 'ull bring the willow-wren,

And then the fust fond nightingale 'ull follow,

A-callin 'Come, dear,' to his laggin hen

Still out at sea, ' the spring is in our glen ;

Come, darlin, wi' the comin o' the swallow.'"

   * Mostly pronounced "kaulo," but sometimes in the
East Midlands "kollo."

And she wur gone!   And then I read the words

In mornin twilight wot you rote to me;

They made the Christmas sing with summer
    birds,

And spring-leaves shine on every frozen tree;

And when the dawnin kindled Rington spire,

Red. And curdlin winter-clouds burnt gold and lollo

Round the dear sun, wot seemed a yolk o' fire,

"Another night," I sez, "has brought him
    nigher;

He's comin wi' the comin o' the swallow."

And soon the bull-pups found me on the Pool—

You know the way they barks to see me slide—

But when the skatin bors o' Rington scool

Comed on, it turned my head to see 'em glide.

I seemed to see you twirlin on your skates,

And somethin made me clap my hans and hollo;

Cutting. "It's him," I sez, "a-chinnin o' them 8s."

But when I woke-like—" I'm the gal wot waits

Alone," I sez, "the comin o' the swallow."

"Comin" seemed ringin in the Christmas-
  chime ;

" Comin" seemed rit on everything I seed,

In beads o' frost along the nets o' rime,

Sparklin on every frozen rush and reed ;

And when the pups began to bark and play,

And frisk and scrabble and bite my frock and
  wallow

Among the snow and fling it up like spray,

I says to them, " You know who rote to say

He's comin wi' the comin o' the swallow.

The thought on't makes the snow-drifts o'
  December

Shine gold," I sez, "like daffodils o' spring

Wot wait beneath: he's comin, pups, remember ;

If not—for me no singin birds 'ull sing :

Cuckoo. No choring chiriklo 'ull hold the gale

Wi' 'Cuckoo, cuckoo,'* over hill and hollow :

There'll be no crakin o' the meadow-rail,

There'll be no ' Jug-jug ' o' the nightingale,

For her wot waits the comin o' the swallow.

Mine own. Come back, minaw, and you may kiss your han

Lady. To that fine rawni rowin on the river ;

Witch. I'll never call that lady a chovihan,

Miserable   Nor yit a mumply gorgie—I'll forgive her.
gentile.

Come back, minaw : I wur to be your wife.

Come back—or, say the word, and I will follow

Your footfalls round the world : I'll leave this

    life

(I've flung away a-ready that 'ere knife)—

I'm dyin for the comin o' the swallow."

    * The gypsies are great observers of the cuckoo, and call certain Spring winds " cuckoo storms," because they bring over the cuckoo earlier than usual.

X

THE FIRST DUKKERIPEN OF THE STARS

(PERCY *on the night of his return to the encampment lingers before calling for the ferry-boat upon the tongue of land called Portobello, and looks down the river, where the stars are brilliantly reflected.* RHONA, *who has secretly come to meet him, appears on the opposite bank, but does not perceive him, owing to the shadowing trees under which he stands.*)

PERCY.

WHAT sees she in the river as it flows?

Does she recall that summer night when we

Rowed here beneath the stars—the night when she,

Unconscious, then, of that within my breast

Which held me mute, murmured in loving jest,

" Our Tarno Rye, he's dreamin while he rows"? Young gentleman.

Or is she gazing at the stars that shine

Mirrored within the stream to read their sign—

Nature's
prophetic
symbol.

The dukkeripen of good or evil made

By their reflections mingled with the shade

Yon pollard willow throws?

That night I murmured, " Life's one joy is this,

To love, to taste the soul's divine delight

Of loving some most lovely soul or sight—

To worship still, though never an answering

sign

Should come from Love asleep within the

shrine."

That night I said, " I ask no more of bliss

Than—while beneath the boat the wavelets

heave—

To touch the gauds upon a gypsy's sleeve,

To see the bright nails shine on glistening

fingers,

To see the throat on which the starlight lingers,

The mouth I dare not kiss."

But that same night Love wrote around the
    prow
  In stars !   Her trembling body turned to me
  In joyful fear of joy, and I could see,
  Pictured in frightened eyes, the blissful things
  A girl's pure soul can see when Love's young
    wings,
Fragrant of heaven and earth, fan first the brow.

      *   *   *   *

    (RHONA *gives a sudden start and looks behind her.*)

  What means that start ?   Why stands she
    there to listen ?
  I see her eyes that in the starlight glisten—
  Her eyes—but not the thing of dread they
    see :
  She's feeling where her knife was wont to
    be—
Ah, would she wore it now !

    (" *The Scollard's* " *figure appears from behind the willow.*)

'Tis he, my gypsy rival, by her side!

He lifts a knife.   She springs, the dauntless

girl,

Lithe as a leopardess!   Ah! can she hurl

The giant down the bank?

(He prepares to plunge into the river in order to swim to
her, when RHONA *meets the onrush of her assailant*
with a blow in the mouth from her fist, which causes
him to totter and then stumble over the bank.)

He falls below,

Falls where the river's darkest waters flow!

Twice, thrice, he rises—sinks beneath the tide!

Only the stars and I have seen him fall.

Gypsy.   Death is her doom who slays a Romany-chal

Gentile.   And weds a gorgio: death!   But only we,

The stars and I who love the slayer, could see

The way the ruffian died.

(He looks in the river, where the reflected stars make
mysterious figures as the ripples twist round the
bulrushes.)

'Twas only we who saw, ye starry throng !

   And one white lie of mine will hide the
      deed

   Of her who gave me love against her
      creed—

   The Romany woman's creed of tribal duty—

   Gave Rhona's wealth of love and faith and
      beauty.

THE STARS WRITE IN THE RIVER.

Falsehood can never shield her : Truth is strong.

PERCY.

   I read your rune : is there no pity, then,

   In Heav'n that wove this net of life for men ?

   Have only Hell and Falsehood heart for
      ruth ?

   Show me, ye mirrored stars, this tyrant
      Truth—

King that can do no wrong !

Ah! Night seems opening! There, above the
  skies,
    Who sits upon that central sun for throne
    Round which a golden sand of worlds is
      strown,
    Stretching right onward to an endless
      ocean,
    Far, far away, of living dazzling motion?
Hearken, King Truth with pictures in thine
  eyes
    Mirrored from gates beyond the furthest
      portal
    Of infinite light, 'tis Love that stands
      immortal,
    The King of Kings. And there on yonder
      bank
    Stands she, and, where the accursed carrion
      sank,
The merry bubbles rise!

At last she sees me on this tongue of
    land ;
    She plunges through the fringe of reed and
        moss,
    She takes the boat; she's pulling straight
        across,
    Startling the moorhens as the dark prow
        brushes
    Through reeds and weeds and water-flags
        and rushes.

       *   *   *   *

Yes, yes, I saw !   Is this the little hand
    That slew him ? How the slender fingers
        quiver
    Against my lips ! Those stars within the
        river
    May write of how he died, but Love, my
        darling,

Looks straight at Doom, though wolves of
Death are snarling,
And smiles : " Behold, I stand ! "

XI

THE PROMISE OF THE SUNRISE

(PERCY *in the tent on the morning after his marriage
with* RHONA *in Gypsy Dell.*)

THE young light peeps through yonder trembling
chink
The tent's mouth makes in answer to a
breeze ;
The rooks outside are stirring in the trees
Thro' which I see the deepening bars of pink.
I hear the earliest anvil's tingling clink
From Jasper's forge ; the cattle on the leas
Begin to low.   She's waking by degrees :
Sleep's rosy fetters melt, but link by link.

What dream is hers ?   Her eyelids shake with
    tears ;
The fond eyes open now like flowers in dew :
She sobs I know not what of passionate fears :
" You'll never leave me now ?   There is but
    you ;
I dreamt a voice was whispering in my ears,
' The Dukkeripen o' stars comes ever true.' "

She rises, startled by a wandering bee
Buzzing around her brow to greet the girl :
She draws the tent wide open with a swirl,
And, as she stands to breathe the fragrancy
Beneath the branches of the hawthorn tree—
Whose dews fall on her head like beads of pearl
Or drops of sunshine firing tress and curl—
The Spirit of the Sunrise speaks to me,
And says, "This bride of yours, I know her well,
And so do all the birds in all the bowers

Who mix their music with the breath of flowers

When greetings rise from river, heath and dell.

See, on the curtain of the morning haze

The Future's finger writes of happy days."

XII

THE MIRRORED STARS AGAIN

(After only a few months with her.)

THE mirrored stars lit all the bulrush-spears,

And all the flags and broad-leaved lily-isles;

The ripples shook the stars to golden smiles,

Then smoothed them back to happy golden

    spheres.

We rowed—we sang; her voice seemed in mine

    ears

An angel's, yet with woman's dearer wiles;

But shadows fell from gathering cloudy piles

And ripples shook the stars to fiery tears.

What shaped those shadows like another boat

Where Rhona sat and he Love made a liar?

There, where the Scollard sank, I saw it float,

While ripples shook the stars to symbols dire;

We wept—we kissed—while starry fingers
  wrote,

And ripples shook the stars to a snake of fire.

XIII

THE PROMISE OF THE SUNRISE RENEWED

(PERCY, *on the anniversary of the mysterious disappearance of* RHONA, *stands in the mouth of his solitary tent in Gypsy Dell. He looks towards the spire of Rington Church in the distance, over which the dawn is gradually brightening into a gorgeous sunrise.*)

DEATH'S year has passed: again the new-
  mown hay,

As on that night, perfumes the Dell—that
  night

E

Whose darkness seemed more dear than
　Eden-light—
Fragrant of Love's warm wings and Love's
　warm breath—
Where here I left her doomed to treacherous
　death
By Romany guile that lured me far away;
　'Twas here—where petals of the morn are
　　cast
　'Mid Night's wild phantoms from the spec-
　　tral past—
　'Twas here she made the vow I smiled at then
　To show her face some morn when hill and
　　glen
Took the first kiss of Day.

But now—not all the starry Virtues seven
　Seem strong as she, nor Time, nor Death, nor
　　Night.

And morning says, " Love hath such godlike
  might
That if the sun, the moon, and all the stars,
Nay, all the spheral spirits who guide their
  cars,
Were quelled by Doom, Love's high-creative
  leaven
Could light new worlds."   If, then, this Lord
  of Fate,
When Death calls in the stars, can re-create,
Is it a madman's dream that Love can show
Rhona, my Rhona, in yon ruby glow,
And build again my heaven ?

" The birds," she said, " they knows us Romany Gypsy girls.
  chies—
Leaseways the gypsy-magpie an the jay— Water-
  wagtail.
They knows the Romany tongue—yis, all we
  say :

So, if the Hernes should do away wi' me
'Cause o' the Scollard's death, the birds will
    see
An' tell the flowers where Rhona's body lies.
    The Scollard's strong to strive wi' now he's
      dead :
    Outside the tent o' nights I hear his tread.
    You mind them stars a-shinin in the river
    That seemed a snake o' fire ?   I see'd you
      shiver :
It had the Scollard's eyes !

But when I'm dead, the Golden Hand o' Love
    Will shine some day where mists o' mornin
      swim ;
    Me too you'll see, dear, when the sun's red
      rim
    Peeps through the Rookery boughs by
      Rington spire,

And makes the wet leaves wink like stars o'
   fire;
Then, when the skylark wakes the thrush and
   dove,
   An' squrrels jump, an' rabbits scrabble roun',
   An' hares cock up their ears a-shinin brown,
   An' grass an' blossoms mix their mornin
   smells
   Wi' Dingle songs from all the chirikels,   Birds.
You'll see me there above."

     *   *   *   *

I think 'twas here—though now I know not
   whether
   Dead joy or living sorrow be the dream—
   In this same tent—round which the branches
   seem
   To stir their whispering leaves as if to tell
   The morn the dreadful secret of the Dell—
I think 'twas here we lived that life together.

*(A shape that at one moment seems like a hand, and
then a feather of gold, appears in the eastern clouds
near the brightening wings of the Spirit of the
Sunrise.)*

My senses mock me : these mad eyes behold

What seems a hand, a mystic hand of gold,

Traced on the steaming canvas of the mist,

Gilding the woof of pearl and amethyst—

A hand or golden feather.

(Beside the Golden Hand RHONA'S *face appears.)*

Is that a picture in a madman's eye?

   Or is it Memory, like a mocking elf,

   Weaving Hope's tapestry to cheat herself ?

   Or does great Nature, she who garners all

   The fleeting pictures Time can limn, recall

The face of her the Romanies doomed to die ?

   Or is there glowing a face from brow to chin

   Where yonder wings of morn are widening

     thin,

Her very face, her throat, her dimpling cheek,

Her mouth—the mouth that love first taught

to speak—

Smiling, " 'Tis I, 'tis I " ?

THE LARK RISING FROM THE HAY-FIELD.

Birds of the Dell, the veils of morn are shaking !

And see the face of her, ye loving birds,

Who knew your songs — who gave them

human words

In those sweet mornings when her breath

would mingle

With breath of flowers, and all the dewy

Dingle

Greeted the Spirit of the Sunrise waking;

Ye birds who saw her buried—ye who know

But cannot utter where she lies below—

Can never tell yon mourner, for the spell

The monstrous deed hath cast about the
Dell—

The man whose heart is breaking !

THE BIRDS OF THE DINGLE.

She keeps her promise, she who made the vow
  No Romany law, no Romany guile, should
    ever
  Divide their lives, nor Death's fell malice sever
  The chain the sunrise forged 'twixt her and
    him ;
  She keeps her promise : see, through mists
    that swim,
Those eyes are hers—that brow is Rhona's
  brow—

Symbol.
  Rhona's, who vowed to show the dukkeripen
  Of Hope, the Golden Hand of promise,
    when

Fate should fulfil the prophet - river's
warning—
Vowed she would gaze from ruby domes of
morning;
She keeps her promise now.

THE SPIRIT OF THE SUNRISE.

Though Love be mocked by Death's obscene
derision,
Love still is Nature's truth and Death her
lie;
Yet hard it is to see the dear flesh die,
To taste the fell destroyer's crowning spite
That blasts the soul with life's most cruel
sight,
Corruption's hand at work in Life's transition:
This sight was spared thee: thou shalt still
retain
Her body's image pictured in thy brain;

The flowers above her weave the only shroud

Thine eye shall see : no stain of Death shall
cloud

Rhona !   Behold the vision !

PERCY.

As on that morn when round our bridal pillow

The sunrise came and you cried : "Smell
the whin ! "

And oped the tent to let the fragrance in,

Yon clouds—like molten metal, boiling brass,

Brightening to gold—are crested as they
pass

With Love's own fire ! — And while each
gleaming billow

Rolls o'er the Dell, 'tis Love's own hand that
launches

The self-same promise through the self-same
branches—

The promise of the Sunrise !—Oak and ash

And birch and elm and thorn pass on the

    flash

Down to the river-willow !

      *   *   *   o   *

XVI

NATURA MALIGNA

(PERCY, *in Norway, and afterwards in the Alps,
whither he has gone to escape the haunting effect of
English scenery upon his mind, has, after living
alone in a log-hut, passed into a state of spiritual
exaltation, and has come to look upon Nature with
the puritanical eyes of a Hindoo Saivite, as being
the malignant foe of Man. And yet the dominant
thought drives him to go every morning to watch for
a sign at sunrise.*)

THE Lady of the Hills with crimes untold

Followed my feet with azure eyes of prey ;

By glacier-brink she stood—by cataract-spray—

When mists were dire, or avalanche-echoes

    rolled.

At night she glimmered in the death-wind
  cold,

And if a footprint shone at break of day,

My flesh would quail, but straight my soul
  would say:

" 'Tis hers whose hand God's mightier hand
  doth hold."

I trod her snow-bridge, for the moon was
  bright,

Her icicle-arch across the sheer crevasse,

When lo, she stood! . . . . God made her let
  me pass,

Then felled the bridge! . . . . Oh, there in
  sallow light,

There down the chasm, I saw her cruel, white,

And all my wondrous days as in a glass.

XVII

THE PROMISE AGAIN RENEWED

(PERCY's *dream in the hut.*)

BENEATH the loveliest dream there coils a fear :

Last night came she whose eyes are memories
    now ;

Her far-off gaze seemed all forgetful how

Love dimmed them once, so calm they shone
    and clear.

"Sorrow," I said, "has made me old, my
    dear ;

'Tis I, indeed, but grief can change the brow :

Beneath *my* load a seraph's neck might bow,

Vigils like mine would blanch an angel's hair."

Oh, then I saw, I saw the sweet lips move !

I saw the love-mists thickening in her eyes—

I heard a sound as if a murmuring dove

Felt lonely in the dells of Paradise ;

But when upon my neck she fell, my love,

Her hair smelt sweet of whin and woodland

spice.

    *   *   o   *   *

    *   *   *   *   *

XX

NATURA BENIGNA

*(The promise of the sunrise on the morning after the
marvellous sight in the sunbow above the cataract.)*

WHAT power is this ? what witchery wins my

feet

To peaks so sheer they scorn the cloaking snow,

All silent as the emerald gulfs below,

Down whose ice-walls the wings of twilight

beat ?

What thrill of earth and heaven—most wild,

most sweet—

What answering pulse that all the senses know,

Comes leaping from the ruddy eastern glow

Where, far away, the skies and mountains

    meet ?

Mother, 'tis I reborn : I know thee well :

That throb I know and all it prophesies,

O Mother and Queen, beneath the olden spell

Of silence, gazing from thy hills and skies !

Dumb Mother, struggling with the years to tell

The secret at thy heart through helpless eyes.

CHRISTMAS AT THE
MERMAID

F

CHRISTMAS AT THE MERMAID

(With the exception of Shakspeare, who has quitted London for good, in order to reside at New Place, Stratford-on-Avon, which he has lately rebuilt, all the members of the Mermaid Club are assembled at the Mermaid Tavern. At the head of the table sits Ben Jonson dealing out the wassail from a large bowl. At the other end sits Raleigh, and at Raleigh's right hand the guest he has brought with him, a stranger, David Gwynn, the Welsh seaman, now an elderly man, whose story of his exploits as a galley-slave in crippling the Armada before it reached the Channel had, years before, whether true or false, given him in the Low Countries a great reputation, the echo of which had reached England. Raleigh's desire was to excite the public enthusiasm for continuing the struggle with Spain on the sea, and generally to revive the fine Elizabethan temper, which had already become almost a thing of the past, save, perhaps, among such choice spirits as those associated with the Mermaid Club.)

CHORUS.

CHRISTMAS knows a merry, merry place,

Where he goes with fondest face,

Brightest eye, brightest hair :

Tell the Mermaid where is that one place :

Where ?

BEN JONSON.

(After filling each cup with wassail.)

Drink first to Stratford Will—belovèd man,

So generous, honest, open, brave and free,

Who merriest at the Apollo used to be—

Merriest of all the merry Falcon clan.

(All drink to " Will Shakspeare.")

CHORUS.

Christmas knows a merry, merry place,

Where he goes with fondest face,

Brightest eye, brightest hair :

Tell the Mermaid where is that one place :

Where ?

BEN JONSON.

That he, the star of revel, bright-eyed Will,

With life at golden summit, fled the town

And took from Thames that light to dwindle

down

O'er Stratford farms, doth make me marvel still.

But, tho' we feast without the king to-night,

The Monarch leaves a regent—friend of friends,

With whose own soul the thronèd spirit

blends

In one fair flame of love's commingling light.

Brother of Shakspeare, wilt thou not rehearse

Those sugared sonnets thy shy muse hath

made,

Those lines where Avon, glassing wood and
glade,
Seems rippling through the sunshine of thy
verse ?

Wilt thou not tell the Mermaid once again,
In golden numbers, what the poet told,
Of how his spirit ever was controlled
By Avon-ripples shining in his brain,

And how those ripples greeted him that day,
Which was the Mermaid's night, when he
the Swan
Flew to the bosom he was nursed upon—
The bosom he so loved when far away ?

Wilt thou not tell us how the river spake
To that sweet Swan returning to its nest
Among the lilies dreaming on the breast
Of Avon, dear to us for Shakspeare's sake ?

CHORUS.

Christmas knows a merry, merry place,

Where he goes with fondest face,

    Brightest eye, brightest hair :

Tell the Mermaid where is that one place :

    Where ?

SHAKSPEARE'S FRIEND.

To sing the nation's song or do the deed

That crowns with richer light the motherland,

Or lend her strength of arm in hour of need

When fangs of foes shine fierce on every hand,

Is joy to him whose joy is working well—

Is goal and guerdon too, though never fame

Should find a thrill of music in his name ;

Yea, goal and guerdon too, though Scorn

    should aim

Her arrows at his soul's high citadel.

But if the fates withhold the joy from me

To do the deed that widens England's day,

Or join that song of Freedom's jubilee

Begun when England started on her way—

Withhold from me the hero's glorious power

To strike with song or sword for her, the

      mother,

And give that sacred guerdon to another,

Him will I hail as my more noble brother—

Him will I love for his diviner dower.

Enough for me who have our Shakspeare's love

To see a poet win the poet's goal,

For Will is he; enough and far above

All other prizes to make rich my soul.

Ben names my numbers golden. Since they

      tell

A tale of him who in his peerless prime

Fled us ere yet one shadowy film of time

Could dim the lustre of that brow sublime,

Golden my numbers are: Ben praiseth well.

THE EVENING AFTER WILL'S RETURN TO
STRATFORD-ON-AVON

As down the bank he strolled through evening
    dew,

Pictures (he told me) of remembered eves

Mixt with that dream the Avon ever weaves,

And all his happy childhood came to view;

He saw a child watching the birds that flew

Above a willow, through whose musky leaves

A green musk-beetle shone with mail and
    greaves

That shifted in the light to bronze and blue.

These dreams, said he, were born of fragrance
    falling

From trees he loved, the scent of musk recalling,

With power beyond all power of things beholden

Or things reheard, those days when elves of
    dusk

Came, veiled the wings of evening feathered
    golden,

And closed him in from all but willow musk.

And then a child beneath a silver sallow—

A child who loved the swans, the moorhens'
    " cheep "—

Angled for bream where river holes were
    deep—

For gudgeon where the water glittered shallow,

Or ate the " fairy cheeses " of the mallow,

And wild fruits gathered where the wavelets
    creep

Round that loved church whose shadow seems
    to sleep

In love upon the stream and bless and hallow ;

And then a child to whom the water-fairies

Sent fish to "bite" from Avon's holes and
　　　shelves,

A child to whom, from richest honey-dairies,

The flower-sprites sent the bees and "sun-
　　　shine elves;"

Then, in the shifting vision's sweet vagaries,

He saw two lovers walking by themselves—

Walking beneath the trees, where drops of rain

Wove crowns of sunlit opal to decoy

Young love from home; and one, the happy
　　　boy,

Knew all the thoughts of birds in every strain—

Knew why the cushat breaks his fond refrain

By sudden silence, "lest his plaint should
　　　cloy"—

Knew when the skylark's changing note of joy

Saith, "Now will I return to earth again"—

Knew every warning of the blackbird's shriek,

And every promise of his joyful song—

Knew what the magpie's chuckle fain would

 speak ;

And, when a silent cuckoo flew along,

Bearing an egg in her felonious beak,

Knew every nest threatened with grievous

 wrong.

He heard her say, " The birds attest our

 troth !

Hark to the mavis, Will, in yonder may

Fringing the sward, where many a hawthorn

 spray

Round summer's royal field of golden cloth

Shines o'er the buttercups like snowy froth,

And that sweet skylark on his azure way,

And that wise cuckoo, hark to what they say :

' We birds of Avon heard and bless you both.'

And, Will, the sunrise, flushing with its glory

River and church, grows rosier with our story!

This breeze of morn, sweetheart, which moves
    caressing,

Hath told the flowers; they wake to lovelier
    growth!

They breathe—o'er mead and stream they
    breathe—the blessing,

'We flowers of Avon heard and bless you
    both!'"

A FRIEND OF MARLOWE'S.

(Who has been sitting moody and silent.)

'Tis when the Christmas joy-bells fill the air

    That memory comes with half-reproachful
    eyes

    To hold before the soul its legacies,

Of grief and joy from Christmas-songs that were.

Friends, friends, there come to me, I know not
why,

  The words I wrote that day my Kit was
slain.

  I would not chill this feast, yet am I fain

To tell of Kit and how I saw him die.

ON SEEING KIT MARLOWE SLAIN
AT DEPTFORD

'Tis Marlowe falls! That last lunge rent
asunder

Our lyre of spirit and flesh, Kit Marlowe's
life,

Whose chords seemed strung by earth and
heav'n at strife,

Yet ever strung to beauty above or under!

Heav'n kens of Man, but oh! the stars can
blunder,

If Fate's hand guided yonder villain's knife

Through that rare brain, so teeming, daring,
　　　rife

With dower of poets — song and love and
　　　wonder.

Or was it Chance?   Shakspeare, who   art
　　　supreme

O'er man and men, yet sharest Marlowe's
　　　sight

To pierce the clouds that hide the inhuman
　　　height

Where man and men and gods and all that
　　　seem

Are Nature's mutterings in her changeful
　　　dream—

Come, spell the runes these bloody rivulets
　　　write!

(They drink in silence to the memory of MARLOWE.*)*

MARLOWE'S FRIEND.

Where'er thou art, "dead Shepherd," look on me;

The boy who loved thee loves more dearly now,

He sees thine eyes in yonder holly-bough;

Oh, Kit, my Kit, the Mermaid drinks to thee!

RALEIGH.

(*Turning to* DAVID GWYNN.)

Wherever billows foam

The Briton fights at home:

His hearth is built of water—water blue and

green;

There's never a wave of ocean

The wind can set in motion

That shall not own our England—own our

England queen.*

* "England is a country that can never be conquered while the Sovereign thereof has the command of the sea."—RALEIGH.

The guest I bring to-night

Had many a goodly fight

On seas the Don hath found—hath found for

    English sails ;

  And once he dealt a blow

  Against the Don to show

What mighty hearts can move—can move in

    leafy Wales.

  Stand up, bold Master Gwynn,

  Who hast a heart akin

To England's own brave hearts—brave hearts

    where'er they beat ;

  Stand up, brave Welshman, thou,

  And tell the Mermaid how

A galley-slave struck hard—struck hard the

    Spanish fleet.

CHORUS.

Christmas knows a merry, merry place.

Where he goes with fondest face,

Brightest eye, brightest hair:

Tell the Mermaid where is that one place:

Where?

DAVID GWYNN'S STORY OF HOW HE AND
THE GOLDEN SKELETON CRIPPLED THE
GREAT ARMADA SAILING OUT

"A GALLEY lie" they called my tale; but he

Whose talk is with the deep kens mighty

tales.

The man, I say, who helped to keep you

free

Stands here, a truthful son of truthful

Wales.

Slandered by England as a loose-lipped liar,

Banished from Ireland, branded rogue and
  thief,
Here stands that Gwynn whose life of
  torments dire
Heaven sealed for England, sealed in blood
  and fire—
  Stands asking here Truth's one reward,
    belief!

And Spain shall tell, with pallid lips of
  dread,
  This tale of mine—shall tell, in future days,
How Gwynn, the galley-slave, once fought and
  bled
  For England when she moved in perilous
    ways;
But say, ye gentlemen of England, sprung
  From loins of men whose ghosts have still
    the sea—

Doth England—she who loves the loudest
  tongue—
Remember mariners whose deeds are sung
  By waves where flowed their blood to keep
    her free?

I see—I see ev'n now—those ships of Spain
  Gathered in Tagus' mouth to make the
    spring;
I feel the cursèd oar, I toil again,
  And trumpets blare, and priests and choir-
    boys sing;
And morning strikes with many a crimson
    shaft,
  Through ruddy haze, four galleys rowing
    out—
Four galleys built to pierce the English craft,
Each swivel-gunned for raking fore and aft,
  Snouted like sword-fish, but with iron snout.

And one we call the *Princess*, one the *Royal*,

    Diana one ; but 'tis the fell *Basana*

Where I am toiling, Gwynn, the true, the

    loyal,

    Thinking of mighty Drake and Gloriana ;

For by their help Hope whispers me that I—

    Whom ten hours' daily travail at a stretch

Has taught how sweet a thing it is to die—

May strike once more where flags of England

    fly,

    Strike for myself and many a haggard

    wretch.

True sorrow knows a tale it may not tell :

    Again I feel the lash that tears my back ;

Again I hear mine own blaspheming yell,

    Answered by boatswain's laugh and scourge's

    crack ;

Again I feel the pang when trying to choke

Rather than drink the wine, or chew the
bread

Wherewith, when rest for meals would break
the stroke,

They cram our mouths while still we sit at
yoke;

Again is Life, not Death, the shape of dread.

By Finisterre there comes a sudden gale,

And mighty waves assault our trembling
galley

With blows that strike her waist as strikes a
flail,

And soldiers cry, "What saint shall bid her
rally?"

Some slaves refuse to row, and some implore

The Dons to free them from the metal tether

By which their limbs are locked upon the
oar;

Some shout, in answer to the billows' roar,

"The Dons and we will drink brine-wine
together."

"Bring up the slave," I hear the captain
cry,

"Who sank the golden galleon *El Dorado*.
The dog can steer."

"Here sits the dog," quoth I,

"Who sank the ship of Commodore
Medrado!"

With hell-lit eyes, blistered by spray and
rain,

Standing upon the bridge, saith he to me:

"Hearken, thou pirate—bold Medrado's bane!—

Freedom and gold are thine, and thanks of
Spain,

If thou canst take the galley through this
sea."

"Ay! ay!" quoth I. The fools unlock me
  straight!
And then 'tis I give orders to the Don,
Laughing within to hear the laugh of Fate,
  Whose winning game I know hath just
  begun.
I mount the bridge when dies the last red
  streak
  Of evening, and the moon seems fain for
  night.
Oh then I see beneath the galley's beak
A glow like Spanish *auto's* ruddy reek—
  Oh then these eyes behold a wondrous
  sight!

A skeleton, but yet with living eyes—
  A skeleton, but yet with bones like gold—
Squats on the galley-beak, in wondrous wise,
  And round his brow, of high imperial mould,

A burning circle seems to shake and shine,

    Bright, fiery bright, with many a living
        gem,

Throwing a radiance o'er the foam-lit brine:

"'Tis God's Revenge," methinks. "Heaven
        sends for sign

    That bony shape—that Inca's diadem."

                  .

At first the sign is only seen of me,

    But well I know that God's Revenge hath
        come

To strike the Armada, set old ocean free,

    And cleanse from stain of Spain the
        beauteous foam.

Quoth I, " How fierce soever be the levin

    Spain's hand can hurl—made mightier still
        for wrong

By that great Scarlet One whose hills are
    seven—

Yea, howsoever Hell may scoff at Heaven—
  Stronger than Hell is God, though Hell is
    strong."

" The dog can steer," I laugh ; " yea, Drake's
    men know
  How sea-dogs hold a ship to Biscay
    waves."
Ah ! when I bid the soldiers go below,
  Some 'neath the hatches, some beside the
    slaves,
And bid them stack their muskets all in
    piles
  Beside the foremast, covered by a sail,
The captives guess my plan — I see their
    smiles
As down the waist the cozened troop defiles,
  Staggering and stumbling landsmen, faint
    and pale.

I say, they guess my plan—to send beneath
  The soldiers to the benches where the
    slaves
Sit, armed with eager nails and eager teeth—
  Hate's nails and teeth more keen than
    Spanish glaives,
Then wait until the tempest's waxing might
  Shall reach its fiercest, mingling sea and
    sky,
Then seize the key, unlock the slaves, and
    smite
The sea-sick soldiers in their helpless plight,
  Then bid the Spaniards pull at oar or die.

Past Ferrol Bay each galley 'gins to stoop,
  Shuddering before the Biscay demon's
    breath.
Down goes a prow—down goes a gaudy poop:
  " The Don's *Diana* bears the Don to death,

Quoth I, "and see the *Princess* plunge and
    wallow
Down purple trough, o'er snowy crest of foam:
See! see! the *Royal,* how she tries to follow
By many a glimmering crest and shimmering
    hollow,
    Where gull and petrel scarcely dare to roam."

Now, three queen-galleys pass Cape Finisterre;
    The Armada, dreaming but of ocean-storms,
Thinks not of mutineers with shoulders bare,
    Chained, bloody-wealed and pale, on
        galley-forms,
Each rower murmuring o'er my whispered plan,
    Deep-burnt within his brain in words of fire,
"Rise, every man, to tear to death his man—
Yea, tear as only galley-captives can,
    When God's Revenge sings loud to ocean's
        lyre."

Taller the spectre grows 'mid ocean's din ;

   The captain sees the Skeleton and pales :

I give the sign : the slaves cry, " Ho for

   Gwynn ! "

   " Teach them," quoth I, " the way we grip in

      Wales."

And, leaping down where hateful boatswains

   shake,

   I win the key — let loose a storm of

      slaves :

" When captives hold the whip, let drivers

   quake,"

They cry ; " sit down, ye Dons, and row for

   Drake,

   Or drink to England's Queen in foaming

      waves."

We leap adown the hatches ; in the dark

   We stab the Dons at random, till I see

A spark that trembles like a tinder-spark,
    Waxing and brightening, till it seems to be
A fleshless skull, with eyes of joyful fire :
    Then, lo! a bony shape with lifted hands—
A bony mouth that chants an anthem dire,
O'ertopping groans, o'ertopping Ocean's quire—
    A skeleton with Inca's diadem stands !

It sings the song I heard an Indian sing,
    Chained by the ruthless Dons to burn at
        stake,
When priests of Tophet chanted in a ring,
    Sniffing man's flesh at roast for Christ His
        sake.
The Spaniards hear : they see : they fight no
        more ;
    They cross their foreheads, but they dare
        not speak.
Anon the spectre, when the strife is o'er,

Melts from the dark, then glimmers as before,
  Burning upon the conquered galley's beak.

And now the moon breaks through the night,
    and shows
  The *Royal* bearing down upon our craft—
Then comes a broadside close at hand, which
    strows
  Our deck with bleeding bodies fore and aft.
I take the helm ; I put the galley near :
  We grapple in silver sheen of moonlit surge.
Amid the *Royal's* din I laugh to hear
The curse of many a British mutineer,
  The crack, crack, crack of boatswain's biting
    scourge.

"Ye scourge in vain," quoth I, " scourging for
    life
  Slaves who shall row no more to save the
    Don ; "

For from the *Royal's* poop, above the strife,

 Their captain gazes at our Skeleton !

" What ! is it thou, Pirate of *El Dorado ?* "

 He shouts in English tongue.   And there,

  behold !

Stands he, the devil's commodore, Medrado.

" Ay ! ay ! " quoth I, " Spain owes me one

  strappado

 For scuttling Philip's ship of stolen

  gold.

" I come for that strappado now," quoth I.

 "What means yon thing of burning bones? "

  he saith.

" 'Tis God's Revenge cries, ' Bloody Spain shall

  die ! '

 The king of El Dorado's name is Death.

 Strike home, ye slaves ; your hour is coming

  swift,"

l cry; "strong hands are stretched to save
    you now;
Show yonder spectre you are worth the gift."
But when the *Royal*, captured, rides adrift,
    I look: the skeleton hath left our prow.

When all are slain, the tempest's wings have
    fled,
    But still the sea is dreaming of the storm:
Far down the offing glows a spot of red,
    My soul knows well it hath that Inca's form.
" It lights," quoth I, "the red cross banner of
    Spain
    There on the flagship where Medina sleeps—
Hell's banner, wet with sweat of Indians'
    pain,
And tears of women yoked to treasure train,
    Scarlet of blood for which the New World
    weeps.

There on the dark the flagship of the Don
  To me seems luminous of the spectre's glow ;
But soon an arc of gold, and then the Sun,
  Rise o'er the reddening billows, proud and
    slow ;
Then, through the curtains of the morning mist,
  That take all shifting colours as they shake,
I see the great Armada coil and twist
Miles, miles along the ocean's amethyst,
  Like hell's old snake of hate—the wingèd
    snake.

And, when the hazy veils of Morn are thinned,
  That snake accursed, with wings which swell
    and puff
Before the slackening horses of the wind,
  Turns into shining ships that tack and luff.
" Behold," quoth I, " their floating citadels,
  The same the priests have vouched for
    musket-proof,

Caracks and hulks and nimble caravels,

That sailed with us to sound of Lisbon bells—

  Yea, sailed from Tagus' mouth, for Christ's
    behoof.

For Christ's behoof they sailed : see how they go

  With that red skeleton to show the way

There sitting on Medina's stem aglow—

  A hundred sail and forty-nine, men say ;

Behold them, brothers, galleon and galeasse—

  Their dizened turrets bright of many a
    plume,

Their gilded poops, their shining guns of brass,

Their trucks, their flags — behold them, how
    they pass—

  With God's Revenge for figurehead — to
    Doom ! "

BEN JONSON.

Now drink to Drake and drink to those

Who when they saw through evening's purple

veils

Two far-divided points that rose—

Two crescent horns that brightened into sails—

Laughed—though methinks their laugh was

grim—

Laughed when those horns like evening's

pinion tips

Burnt ruddier, and the centre dim

Came up and filled the horizon's rim—

Laughed loud and cried: "See how the pirzes

swim,

Our Spanish ships"—

The men who saw the Armada float,

And lit the beacon fires to spread the news,

While smack, and hoy, and fishing boat

Swelled big with pride, and landsmen joined
    the crews.

Papist like Lutheran met with laughter

The ban of Rome—-Drink to those Papist halls

    That rang with shouts from rush to rafter,

    "Whate'er the bans the winds may waft
      her,

England's true men are we and Pope's men
    after,

        When England calls."

DRAYTON.

Fill every cup with Mermaid-sack,

And sing a song of Drake and Howard's men,

    Who broke the Spanish Bloodhound's back

In England's glorious week of triumph, when

    Her fate, which aye was Freedom's fate,

Hung on the sons she suckled to be free—

When down before them in the Strait

Went that fell flag the free waves hate,

And God said: " England, this is thine estate!

And gave the sea.

CHORUS.

The sea !

Thus did England fight ;

And shall not England smite

With Drake's strong stroke in battles yet to be ?*

And while the winds have power

Shall England lose the dower

She won in that great hour—

The sea ?

* He who alive to them a Dragon was
    Shalbe a Dragon unto them againe,
For with his death his terrour shall not passe,
    But still amid the aire he shall remaine.
            Sir Francis Drake, by CHARLES FITZGEOFFREY
                    Oxford, 1596.

BEN JONSON.

(*Turning to* RALEIGH.)

To win the Theban prize, each brought his
    lay,
  When, lo! a stranger stood, wind-flushed
    and tanned,
  Who sang of marvellous sights in many a land
And voices heard on waters far away.

But fools shall give to fools the bay for prize,
  Yea, though Apollo's self hath brought an
    ode :
  And songs are sung in Time's forgotten mode
When high gods sing from still-receding skies.

The bard whose song the Thebans might not
    follow,
  Because he sang of more than Theban things,

Was he whose music, struck from Nature's
strings,
Builded the walls of Ilion, great Apollo.

Cried Phœbus, soaring high—his bright feet
shod
With Day that quenched the day and hid the
town—
" Ye spurn Apollo as a sunburnt clown,
Ye pallid priestlings of a sunburnt god !

" The milk-white forehead, tender and dainty-
skinned,
Your sculptors give me—lips too fine to
quaff
The wine of morning — make Olympus
laugh :
Gods know the sun-god bronzed by brine and
wind."

The Mermaid, "Ocean-shepherd," drinks to thee:

    Sunburnt thou art, and knowest the great

        round world,

    As Phœbus knows: tell us how England hurled

Spain to the bottom of the guardian sea.

CHORUS.

Christmas knows a merry, merry place,

Where he goes with fondest face,

    Brightest eye, brightest hair:

Tell the Mermaid where is that one place:

    Where?

RALEIGH.

    Hail to the wassail-steam that rises

Above the head of him who brewed it, Ben.

    Rare shapes it takes and wondrous guises

Of ships, and flags, and guns, and fighting

    men.

The Mermaid's spicy steam to-night
Brings back the curling clouds of other smoke—
    Less dainty of scent, less pure and white,
    Yet sweet and full of high delight
To me who saw how English sailors fight
        On English oak.

    I feel the west wind blowing in,
And, when out-warps the fleet of every sail,
    I hear Drake say, "'Twill soon begin,
The game between the sword-fish and the
      whale "—
    Hear Wynter say: " Those galleons towered,
With Philip's trinkets, Philip's filigree,
    And painted trucks and pennons flowered,
    Shall feel the stroke of England's Howard,
And touch the ships of Drake whose keels
      have scoured
        Philip's own sea."

CHORUS.

The sea !

Thus did England fight ;

And shall not England smite

With Drake's strong stroke in battles yet to be ?

And while the winds have power

Shall England lose the dower

She won in that great hour—

The sea ?

RALEIGH.

Out-warp the ships the Spaniard knew

Ere Drake returned from " singeing Philip's
beard,"

With flags that under Cadiz flew

When right between the Spanish keels he
steered ;

Out-warp the ships John Hawkins made—

Hornets for golden bees from El Dorado—

    With keels as fine as rapier-blade,

    Slipping to follow or evade

As swiftly through a Spanish cannonade

        As sea-gull's shadow.

    Off Plymouth Sound the Sabbath smiles

When whale and swordfish meet in deadly

        play—

    When up the Channel, miles on miles,

The swordfish stabs and stabs and glides away.

    The Spaniard hath both sail and oar.

And what hath England ? Sons who strike

        with glee

    To music of the cannon's roar—

    Strike, strike till e'en the rooks on shore

    Rise scared, and Channel sea-fowls wheel and

    soar

        Right out to sea.

CHORUS.

The sea !

Thus did England fight ;

And shall not England smite

With Drake's strong stroke in battles yet to be ?

And while the winds have power

Shall England lose the dower

She won in that great hour—

The sea ?

RALEIGH.

And now from bays and creeks and coves,

Through all the sacred ways, from farthest
    Scillies

To that sweet bay where whispering groves

Stretch on to many a lawn of Jersey lilies ;

From Lyme to that flower-fragrant home

Of nightingale and rose, beloved Wight,

They come—in smacks, in skiffs they come—
And even in little shallops some—
To show how foes who brave our Channel-foam
Will have to fight.

When, like a playful hound released,
From purple portals of the opening day
At last the wind from out the east
Drives smoke and vapour over Weymouth Bay,
Medina hath the wind, he sees,
And bears on Howard's line with luckless
might;
And Drake knows well the Narrow Seas
That nurtured him—knows how the breeze
Of summer follows all the sun's decrees
From dawn till night.

At last Medina finds his goal,
And, safe as hunted wolf within his lair,

He anchors close by Calais shoal,

While England's sea-dogs fret around him
  there.

" Damned be the foe who will not fight!"

Saith Wynter. "List, my Lord High Admiral ;

  Beneath yon moon a-shining bright

  There lies the Don in direst plight,

With riddled hulls and sails—with men in
  fright,

        But fight he shall.

" O' nights, my lord, the tide sets down

To where yon gaudy-bellied gold-tubs lie

  So close they seem like Plymouth town

Save for the lanterns swaying there on high.

  When midnight sounds by Spanish bells,

To-morrow night, before the moon shines free,

  Send fire-ships round their caravels,

  Their clumsy galleon-citadels ;

The Don will deem them 'Antwerp's floating
hells'

That burn on sea."

CHORUS.

The sea!

Thus did England fight ;

And shall not England smite

With Drake's strong stroke in battles yet to be ?

And while the winds have power

Shall England lose the dower

She won in that great hour—

The sea?

RALEIGH.

The midnight bells! I hear them rung !

In strength the Spaniard sleeps, but battle-
thinned ;

No dreams hath he of Prowse and Young,

There stealing with the fire-ships down the
wind,

Till smoke up-curls and flames devour

And Night's black wings are glowing like fiery
pinions,

Which wax in light and wax in power,

Illuming Gravelines wakened tower

With sparks and flakes that seem a ruddy
shower

From hell's dominions.

Troops, priests, and sailors dance with dread,

As dance bewildered steeds in burning stables ;

Sails open in the reeking red :

The Fleet Invincible hath slipped its cables !

" The Antwerp fire ! the floating mine ! "

The Spaniards shout. But now there comes to me

A sign I know, the Channel's sign—

I

A sound most like the sleuth hound's whine

When slot is found : Drake knows that cry

    divine :

        'Tis England's sea !

CHORUS.

      The sea !

Thus did England fight ;

And shall not England smite

With Drake's strong stroke in battles yet to be ?

  And while the winds have power

  Shall England lose the dower

  She won in that great hour—

      The sea ?

RALEIGH.

Six miles from shore lies trembling Spain,

Yearning for Calais Roads and Flushing sands ;

But Drake hath said, "Never again

Shall Parma with the Golden Duke shake

    hands."

The south-west wind has never shifted,

And there, while morning opes bewildered eyes,

    While Spain lies shattered, scattered, drifted,

    With hulls and sails the balls have rifted,

Both warring fleets as by a hand are lifted—

    Our billows rise !

    While morning gazes o'er the waves,

Gilding the ships, the Spaniards sallow-skinned,

    The cruel oars, the weary slaves,

Drake starts : "What signs are these on sea

    and wind ?"

    He knows what glorious combatant

Is moving now to hold our England free ;

    He knows our Channel's covenant

    With Freedom—knows how billows pant,

Ere yet begins the Channel's English chant
　　　Of wind and sea.

CHORUS.

　　The sea!

　Thus did England fight;

　And shall not England smite

With Drake's strong stroke in battles yet to be?

　And while the winds have power

　Shall England lose the dower

　She won in that great hour—

　　The sea?

RALEIGH.

The choirboys sing the matin song,

When down falls Seymour on the Spaniard's
　　　right.

He drives the wing—a huddled throng—

Back on the centre ships, that steer for flight.

   While galleon hurtles galeasse,

And oars that fight each other kill the slaves,

   As scythes cut down the summer grass,

   Drake closes on the writhing mass,

Through which the balls at closest ranges pass,

      Skimming the waves.

   Fiercely do galley and galeasse fight,

Running from ship to ship like living things.

   With oars like legs, with beaks that smite,

Winged centipedes they seem with tattered

      wings.

   Through smoke we see their chiefs encased

In shining mail of gold where blood congeals ;

   And once I see within a waist

   Wild English captives ashen-faced,

Their bending backs by Spanish scourges laced

      In purple weals.

(David Gwynn *here leaps up, pale and panting, and
bares a scarred arm, but at a sign from* Raleigh
sits down again.)

The Don fights well, but fights not now

The cozened Indian whom he kissed for friend,

To pluck the gold from off the brow,

Then fling the flesh to priests to burn and
rend.

He hunts not now the Indian maid

With bloodhound's bay — Peru's confiding
daughter,

Who saw in flowery bower or glade

The stranger's god-like cavalcade,

And worshipped, while he planned Pizarro's
trade

Of rape and slaughter.

His fight is now with Drake and Wynter,

Hawkins, and Frobisher, and English fire,

Bullet and cannon ball and splinter,

Till every deck gleams, greased with bloody

   mire :

   Heaven smiles to see that battle wage,

Close battle of musket, carabine, and gun :

   Oh, vainly doth the Spaniard rage

   Like any wolf that tears his cage !

'Tis English sails shall win the weather gauge

   Till set of sun !

   Their troops, superfluous as their gold,

Out-numbering all their seamen two to one,

   Are packed away in every hold—

Targets of flesh for every English gun—

   Till, like Pizarro's halls of blood,

Or slaughter-pens where swine or beeves are

   pinned,

   Lee-scuppers pour a crimson flood,

   Reddening the waves for many a rood,

As eastward, eastward still the galleons scud
Before the wind.

" Doth mighty Parma wait to join
The ' deathless fleet ' that holds four thousand
dead ?
That fleet shall never turn the Groyne
If cannon-gear be ours and sailors' bread."
As thus he speaks brave Cumberland
Sweeps down to set the crown on Victory ;
While privateers on every hand
Are flocking, flocking, from the land,
To drive out Philip's Pope-anointed band
To the open sea.

CHORUS.

The sea!

Thus did England fight ;
And shall not England smite

With Drake's strong stroke in battles yet to be?

And while the winds have power

Shall England lose the dower

She won in that great hour—

The sea ?

BEN JONSON.

(At the conclusion of RALEIGH'S *song.)*

Sweet is the song of victories

Which only leaves the singer's deed unsung.

(He stops, having perceived that GWYNN, *who has been
following* RALEIGH'S *story with intense excitement,
has now passed into a condition resembling hysteria,
staring into the air and pulling open his dress to
display scars of the branding iron and of the
boatswain's galley-scourge.)*

Look to thy friend !   Before his eyes

What ghostly picture in the air is hung ?

LODGE.

Good Master Gwynn, we pray thee tell
The Mermaid what hath blanched thy lips and
    brow.

DEKKER.

Some sight he sees of Death or Hell.

CHAPMAN.

We marvel, friend, what mighty spell,
Making each vein upon thy forehead swell,
        Hath seized thee now.

GWYNN.

With towering sterns, with golden stems
That totter in the smoke before their foe,
    I see them pass the mouth of Thames,
With death above the billows, death below !

Who leads them down the tempest's path,

From Thames to Yare, from Yare to Tweed-

    mouth blown,

  Past many a Scottish hill and strath,

  All helpless in the wild wind's wrath,

Each mainmast stooping, creaking like a lath ?

    The Skeleton !

  At length with toil the cape is passed,

And faster and faster still the billows come

  To coil and boil till every mast

Is flecked with clinging flakes of snowy foam.

  I see, I see, where galleons pitch,

That Inca's bony shape burn on the waves,

  Flushing each emerald scarp and ditch,

  While Mother Carey, Orkney's witch,

  Waves to the Spectre's song her lantern-

    switch

      O'er ocean-graves.

The glimmering crown of Scotland's head
They pass. No foe dares follow but the storm.
The Spectre, like a sunset red,
Illumines mighty Wrath's defiant form,
    And makes the dreadful granite peak
Burn o'er the ships with brows of prophecy;
    Yea, makes that silent countenance speak
    Above the tempest's foam and reek,
More loud than all the loudest winds that
        shriek,

        " Tyrants, ye die ! "

The Spectre, by the Orkney Isles,
Writes " God's Revenge " on waves that climb
        and dash,
    Foaming right up the sand-built piles,
Where ships are hurled.   It sings amid the
        crash ;
    Yea, sings amid the tempest's roar,

Snapping of ropes, cracking of spars set
    free,
  And yells of captives chained to oar,
  And cries of those who strike for shore,
"Spain's murderous breath of blood shall foul
    no more
      The righteous sea!"

BEN JONSON.

So lists the Mermaid to the sailor's song,*
  But let not wassail cool on Christmas
    Eve :
  The hero's tale being told, why, let us
    leave
For merrier themes the fight of Right with
    Wrong.

---

* " So lists the sailor to the mermaid's song."—*Arden of Feversham.*

WASSAIL CHORUS.

CHORUS.

CHRISTMAS knows a merry, merry place.

Where he goes with fondest face,

Brightest eye, brightest hair :

Tell the Mermaid where is that one place :

Where ?

RALEIGH.

'Tis by Devon's glorious halls,

Whence, dear Ben, I come again :

Bright with golden roofs and walls—

El Dorado's rare domain—

Seem those halls when sunlight launches

Shafts of gold through leafless branches,

Where the winter's feathery mantle blanches

Field and farm and lane.

CHORUS.

Christmas knows a merry, merry place.

Where he goes with fondest face,

Brightest eye, brightest hair :

Tell the Mermaid where is that one place:

Where ?

DRAYTON.

'Tis where Avon's wood-sprites weave

Through the boughs a lace of rime.

While the bells of Christmas Eve

Fling for Will the Stratford-chime

O'er the river-flags embossed

Rich with flowery runes of frost—

O'er the meads where snowy tufts are

tossed—

Strains of olden time.

CHORUS.

Christmas knows a merry, merry place,

Where he goes with fondest face,

Brightest eye, brightest hair :

Tell the Mermaid where is that one place :

Where ?

SHAKSPEARE'S FRIEND.

'Tis, methinks, on any ground

Where our Shakspeare's feet are set.

There smiles Christmas, holly-crowned

With his blithest coronet :

Friendship's face he loveth well :

'Tis a countenance whose spell

Sheds a balm o'er every mead and dell

Where we used to fret.

CHORUS.

Christmas knows a merry, merry place,

Where he goes with fondest face,

Brightest eye, brightest hair :

Tell the Mermaid where is that one place:

Where ?

HEYWOOD.

More than all the pictures, Ben,

Winter weaves by wood or stream,

Christmas loves our London, when

Rise thy clouds of wassail-steam—

Clouds like these, that, curling, take

Forms of faces gone, and wake

Many a lay from lips we loved, and make

London like a dream.

K

CHORUS.

Christmas knows a merry, merry place,

Where he goes with fondest face,

Brightest eye, brightest hair:

Tell the Mermaid where is that one place:

Where?

BEN JONSON.

Love's old songs shall never die,

Yet the new shall suffer proof;

Love's old drink of Yule brew I,

Wassail for new love's behoof:

Drink the drink I brew, and sing

Till the berried branches swing,

Till our song make all the Mermaid ring—

Yea, from rush to roof.

FINALE.

Christmas loves this merry, merry place :—

Christmas saith with fondest face

Brightest eye, brightest hair :

" Ben ! the drink tastes rare of sack and mace :

Rare ! "

A TALK ON WATERLOO
BRIDGE

THE LAST SIGHT OF GEORGE BORROW

WE talked of " Children of the Open Air,"

Who once on hill and valley lived aloof,

Loving the sun, the wind, the sweet reproof

Of storms, and all that makes the fair earth

     fair,

Till, on a day, across the mystic bar

Of moonrise, came the " Children of the

     Roof,"

Who find no balm 'neath evening's rosiest

     woof,

Nor dews of peace beneath the Morning Star

We looked o'er London, where men wither and
    choke,

Roofed in, poor souls, renouncing stars and
    skies,

And lore of woods and wild wind prophecies,

Yea, every voice that to their fathers spoke:

And sweet it seemed to die ere bricks and
    smoke

Leave never a meadow outside Paradise.

MISCELLANEOUS POEMS

MISCELLANEOUS POEMS

A DEAD POET

Thou knewest that island, far away and lone,
    Whose shores are as a harp, where billows
        break
    In spray of music and the breezes shake
O'er spicy seas a woof of colour and tone,
While that sweet music echoes like a moan
    In the island's heart, and sighs around the
        lake,
    Where, watching fearfully a watchful snake,
A damsel weeps upon her emerald throne.

Life's ocean, breaking round thy senses' shore,
   Struck golden song, as from the strand of
      Day :
For us the joy, for thee the fell foe lay—
Pain's blinking snake around the fair isle's core,
   Turning to sighs the enchanted sounds that
      play
Around thy lovely island evermore.

A GRAVE BY THE SEA

I

Yon sightless poet* whom thou leav'st behind,
  Sightless and trembling like a storm-struck
    tree,
  Above the grave he feels but cannot see,
Save with the vision Sorrow lends the
    mind,
Is he indeed the loneliest of mankind ?
  Ah no !—For all his sobs, he seems to me
  Less lonely standing there, and nearer thee,
Than I—less lonely, nearer—standing blind !

* Philip Bourke Marston.

Free from the day, and piercing Life's disguise
  That needs must partly enveil true heart
    from heart,
  His inner eyes may see thee as thou art
In Memory's land—see thee beneath the
    skies
Lit by thy brow—by those beloved eyes,
  While I stand by him in a world apart.

II

I stand like her who on the glittering Rhine
  Saw that strange swan which drew a faëry
    boat
  Where shone a knight whose radiant fore-
    head smote
Her soul with light and made her blue eyes
    shine

For many a day with sights that seemed divine,

  Till that false swan returned and arched his

    throat

  In pride, and called him, and she saw him

    float

Adown the stream : I stand like her and pine.

I stand like her, for she, and only she,

Might know my loneliness for want of thee.

  Light swam into her soul, she asked not

    whence,

Filled it with joy no clouds of life could

    smother,

  And then, departing like a vision thence,

Left her more lonely than the blind, my brother.

III

Last night Death whispered : "Death is but
    the name
  Man gives the Power which lends him life
    and light,
  And then, returning past the coast of night,
Takes what it lent to shores from whence it
    came."
What balm in knowing the dark doth but
    reclaim
  The sun it lent, if day hath taken flight ?
  Art thou not vanished—vanished from my
    sight—
Though somewhere shining, vanished all the
    same ?

With Nature dumb, save for the billows' moan,
  Engirt by men I love, yet desolate—

Standing with brothers here, yet dazed and
    lone,
  King'd by my sorrow, made by grief so
    great
That man's voice murmurs like an insect's
    drone—
  What balm, I ask, in knowing that Death is
    Fate ?

IV

Last night Death whispered : " Life's purblind
    procession,
  Flickering with blazon of the human story—
  Time's fen-flame over Death's dark terri-
    tory—
Will leave no trail, no sign of Life's aggres-
    sion.

Yon moon that strikes the pane, the stars in
    session,
  Are weak as Man they mock with fleeting
    glory.
  Since Life is only Death's frail feudatory,
How shall love hold of Fate in true possession ?"

I answered thus : " If Friendship's isle of palm
  Is but a vision, every loveliest leaf,
Can knowledge of its mockery soothe and calm
  This soul of mine in this most fiery grief ?
  If Love but holds of Life through Death in
    fief,
What balm in knowing that Love is Death's—
    what balm ?

V

Yea, thus I boldly answered Death—even I
  Who have for boon—who have for deathless
    dower—
  Thy love, dear friend, which broods, a magic
    power,
Filling with music earth and sea and sky:
" O Death," I said, "not Love, but thou shalt
    die;
  For, this I know, though thine is now the
    hour,
  And thine these angry clouds of doom that
    lour,
Death striking Love but strikes to deify."

Yet while I spoke I sighed in loneliness,
For strange seemed Man, and Life seemed
    comfortless,

L

And night, whom we two loved, seemed
    strange and dumb ;
And, waiting till the dawn the promised sign,
I watched—I listened for that voice of thine,
    Though Reason said : " Nor voice nor face
    can come."

BIRCHINGTON, EASTERTIDE 1882

THE OMNIPOTENCE OF LOVE

I

THE SLAVE GIRL'S PROGRESS TO PARADISE*

(Beneath the cypress overhanging her lover's tomb the slave girl lies stretched on the stone. In the shadow by the tree are seen the "wide black eyes" and the sombre wings of Azrael, the Angel of Death.)

THE SLAVE GIRL.

ANGEL of Death! Hearken in yonder wood

How turtle and nightingale are murmuring

"Pity";

* Although the Koran refers three times to the wives of the just accompanying them into Paradise (Sura xiii. 36-42), and although there is a tradition of a Paradise apart from the men reserved for the few women whom Mohammed did not see in his vision of perdition, the popular notion in some Mohammedan countries is that women have no souls to be either blessed or damned.

"Pity," yon slave-girls moan who brought me
    food
And milk and shawls, to soothe my solitude :
    See how they weep, returning to the city.

(ILYÀS THE PROPHET, *who is passing the tomb, stops
    to listen.*)

ILYÀS.

What sorrow, child, hath made thee fain to
    die ?

THE SLAVE GIRL.

I would not die : this frame of mine remem-
    bers
Each touch of his which gave it sanctity,
Flickering within the body's memory,
    As come and go the sparks in slumbering
        embers.

Save me from Azraeel—him whose sword
　　divides
　Love's dearest bonds—whose malice struck
　　to sever
My life from one who loves me, though he
　　bides
Where never slave girl stood, with houri brides.
　I would not die, but live and weep for ever.

ILYÀS TO AZRAEEL.

Yea, Love is strong! This child would spend
　　her days
　Here on this tomb with cypress boughs for
　　cover,
While travellers whisper as they stop and gaze
Across the graveyard, "See how love can craze!
　She lives upon the tomb where sleeps her
　　lover."

THE SLAVE GIRL.

Death knows I have no soul, and never more

  Those lips shall touch the widowed lips that

    quiver

With memories of the light which once they

    wore.

Death knows I have no soul with wings to

    soar

  To one who stands beside the Holy river.

*(A spirit resembling the slave girl herself in form and
feature, but winged like a Peri, descends from the
sunset clouds, leaving an iridescent track behind it.)*

ILYÀS TO AZRAEEL.

Lo! Allah sends a vision down the air

  That   leaves   a   rainbow   track   o'er   thy

    dominions.

THE SLAVE GIRL.

What shape is that which treads the Peris'
    stair ?

It stands beside me now with shining hair,

    I breathe the musk of Aidenn from its
        pinions.

ILYλS.

No soulless Peri this whose eyes illume

    With mirrored radiance of a deathless
        glory

The cypress branches round thy lover's
    tomb,

And flush the vans of Death with such a
    bloom

    That Evening's rosy wings seem wan and
        hoary.

THE SLAVE GIRL TO THE VISION.

Spirit, whose tears are falling on the stone,

  Doth sorrow stamp an angel's forehead

    human ?

Thou speakest not, but as a sight half known,

Within a dream, thy face seems like mine

  own,

  And eyes that weep must needs be kin to

    woman.

AZRAEEL.

Thy lover waiteth by the Holy Lote.

THE SLAVE GIRL.

With houris ?

AZRAEEL.

Nay, he loveth still a maiden.

THE SLAVE GIRL.

That maiden hath no soul to ford the moat.

ILYÀS.

Thou'rt loved of Allah!

THE SLAVE GIRL.

Yet his servant smote

Him whom the houris dare not clasp in
Aidenn.

(The spirit stoops and kisses the slave girl's forehead.)

ILYÀS.

I think the spirit's kiss upon thy brow
Seals Allah's promise of a blissful morrow.

THE SLAVE GIRL TO THE VISION.

Morrow for me! Speak, spirit, who art thou?

ILYÀS.

'Tis thine own soul—the spirit with thee now

　　Is thine own soul new-lit by love and

　　sorrow.

II

THE BEDOUIN-CHILD

(*Among the Bedouins a father in enumerating his
children never counts his daughters, for a daughter
is considered a disgrace.*)

ILYÀS the prophet, lingering 'neath the moon,

　　Heard from a tent a child's heart-withering

　　wail,

　　Mixt with the message of the nightingale,

And, entering, found, sunk in mysterious

　　swoon,

A little maiden dreaming there alone.

　　She babbled of her father sitting pale

'Neath wings of Death—'mid sights of

    sorrow and bale,

And pleaded for his life in piteous tone.

" Poor child, plead on," the succouring prophet

    saith,

    While she, with eager lips, like one who

        tries

    To kiss a dream, stretches her arms and

        cries

To Heaven for help—" Plead on ; such pure

    love-breath,

Reaching the Throne, might stay the wings of

    Death

    That, in the Desert, fan thy father's eyes."

The drouth-slain camels lie on every hand ;

    Seven sons await the morning vultures'

        claws ;

'Mid empty water-skins and camel-maws

The father sits, the last of all the band.

He mutters, drowsing o'er the moonlit sand,

"Sleep fans my brow: Sleep makes us all

pashas;

Or, if the wings are Death's, why Azraeel

draws

A childless father from an empty land."

"Nay," saith a Voice, "the wind of Azraeel's

wings

A child's sweet breath hath stilled; so God

decrees":—

A camel's bell comes tinkling on the breeze,

Filling the Bedouin's brain with bubble of

springs

And scent of flowers and shadow of wavering

trees

Where, from a tent, a little maiden sings.

JOHN THE PILGRIM

A.D. 1249

THE MIRAGE

BENEATH the sand-storm John the Pilgrim
    prays ;
  But when he rises, lo! an Eden smiles,
  Green leafy slopes, meadows of chamomiles,
Claspt in a silvery river's winding maze :
"Water, water! Blessed be God!" he says,
  And totters gasping toward those happy
    isles.
  Then all is fled! Over the sandy piles
The bald-eyed vultures come and stand at
    gaze.

"God heard me not," says he, "blessed be
   God!"

   And dies. But as he nears the pearly
      strand,

   Heav'n's outer coast where waiting angels
      stand,

He looks below: "Farewell, thou hooded clod,

   Brown corpse the vultures tear on bloody
      sand:

God heard my prayer for life—blessed be
   God!"

COLUMBUS

FOR THE FESTIVAL AT HUELVA

A Castilla y a Leon
Nuevo Mundo dió Colon.

To Christ he cried to quell Death's deafening
measure
　Sung by the storm to Death's own chartless
　sea ;
　To Christ he cried for glimpse of grass or
　tree
When, hovering o'er the calm, Death watched
　at leisure ;
And when he showed the men, now dazed
　with pleasure,

Faith's new world glittering star-like on the
    lee,
" I trust that by the help of Christ," said he,
" I presently shall light on golden treasure."

What treasure found he ? Chains and pains
    and sorrow—
    Yea, all the wealth those noble seekers find
    Whose footfalls mark the music of mankind !
'Twas his to lend a life : 'twas Man's to borrow :
'Twas his to make, but not to share, the
    morrow
    Who in Love's memory lives this morn en-
    shrined.

BEATRICE

FOR THE SIXTH CENTENARY OF BEATRICE'S DEATH,

COMMEMORATED AT FLORENCE IN MAY, 1890

THOU, spreading through six hundred years an
air
Of memory fresh as Morning's altar-spice,
Thou, Star of Dante—Star of Paradise,
Hast made the star of womanhood more fair;
For though thou art now his lofty guardian
there,
Victress o'er jealous Sin, who dared entice
His feet from thee *—though now the high
device

* "Purg.," c. xxx. See also Guido Cavalcanti's sonnet
to Dante Alighieri, rebuking his way of life after the death
of Beatrice.

M

Of wisdom lights the wreath around thine
     hair;
Those eyes can dim the angels' eyes above
   Because they tell what flight was thine
    below :
   No eagle-flight past peaks of fire and snow,
But through Life's leaves the flutter of a dove
Whose beating wings soothed Dante's air with
   love—
   Struck music from the wind of Dante's woe.

THE THREE FAUSTS

INSCRIBED TO MISS ELEONORE D'ESTERRE KEELING

I

THE MUSIC OF HELL

I HAD a dream of wizard harps of hell

Beating through starry worlds a pulse of pain

That held them shuddering in a fiery spell,

Yea, spite of all their songs—a fell refrain

Which, leaping from some red orchestral sun,

Through constellations and through eyeless
     space

Sought some pure core of bale, and finding
     one

(An orb whose shadows flickering on her face

Seemed tragic shadows from some comic mime,

Incarnate visions mouthing hopes and fears

That Fate was playing to the Fiend of Time),

Died in a laugh 'mid oceanic tears :

" Berlioz," I said, " thy strong hand makes me
  weep,

That God did ever wake a world from sleep."

II

THE MUSIC OF EARTH

I had a dream of golden harps of earth :

And when they shook the web of human life,

The warp of sorrow and the weft of mirth,

Divinely trembling in a blissful strife,

Seemed answering in a dream that master-
  song

Which built the world and lit the holy skies.

Oh, then my listening soul waxed great and
    strong
Till my flesh trembled at her high replies!
But when the web seemed answering lower
    strings
Which hymn the temple at the god's expense,
And bid the soul fly low on fleshly wings
To gather dews—rich honey-dews of sense,
" Gounod," I said, " I love that siren-breath,
Though with it chimes the throbbing heart of
    Death."

III

THE MUSIC OF HEAVEN

I had a dream of azure harps of heaven
Beating through starry worlds a pulse of
    joy,

Quickening the light with Love's electric
    leaven,
Quelling Death's hand, uplifted to destroy,
Building the rainbow there with tears of man
High over hell, bright over Night's abysses,
The arc of sorrow in a smiling span
Of tears of many a lover's dying kisses,
And tears of many a Gretchen's towering
    sorrow,
And many a soul fainting for dearth of kin,
And many a soul that hath but night for
    morrow,
And many a soul that hath no day but sin ;
"Schumann," I said, "thine is a wondrous
    story
Of tears so bright they dim the seraphs'
    glory."

TOAST TO OMAR KHAYYÀM

AN EAST ANGLIAN ECHO-CHORUS

INSCRIBED TO OLD OMARIAN FRIENDS IN MEMORY OF
HAPPY DAYS BY OUSE AND CAM

CHORUS.

In this red wine, where Memory's eyes seem
    glowing,
  And days when wines were bright by Ouse
    and Cam,
And Norfolk's foaming nectar glittered,
    showing
What beard of gold John Barleycorn was
    growing,
We drink to thee, right heir of Nature's
    knowing,

Omar Khayyàm !

I

Star-gazer, who canst read, when Night is
strowing
  Her scriptured orbs on Time's wide ori-
  flamme,
  Nature's proud blazon: "Who shall bless or
  damn?
Life, Death, and Doom are all of my bestowing!"
      CHORUS: Omar Khayyàm!

II

Poet, whose stream of balm and music, flowing
  Through Persian gardens, widened till it
  swam—
  A fragrant tide no bank of Time shall dam—
Through Suffolk meads, where gorse and may
  were blowing,
      CHORUS: Omar Khayyàm!

III

Who blent thy song with sound of cattle
    lowing,
  And caw of rooks that perch on ewe and ram,
  And hymn of lark, and bleat of orphan lamb,
And swish of scythe in Bredfield's dewy
    mowing ?
           CHORUS : Omar Khayyàm !

IV

'Twas Fitz, "Old Fitz," whose knowledge,
    farther going
  Than lore of Omar, "Wisdom's starry
    Cham,"
Made richer still thine opulent epigram :
Sowed seed from seed of thine immortal
    sowing.
           CHORUS: Omar Khayyàm

In this red wine, where Memory's eyes seem
   glowing,
  And days when wines were bright by Ouse
    and Cam,
And Norfolk's foaming nectar glittered,
   showing
What beard of gold John Barleycorn was
   growing,
We drink to thee till, hark! the cock is
   crowing!

               Omar Khayyàm!

PRAYER TO THE WINDS

ON PLANTING AT THE HEAD OF FITZGERALD'S
GRAVE TWO ROSE-TREES WHOSE ANCESTORS
HAD SCATTERED THEIR PETALS OVER THE
TOMB OF OMAR KHAYYÀM

*" My tomb shall be on a spot where the north-wind
may strow roses upon it."* — OMAR KHAYYÀM *to*
KWÁJAH NIZAMI.

HEAR us, ye winds!

  From where the north-wind strows

Blossoms that crown "the King of Wisdom's " tomb,

The trees here planted bring remembered
 bloom,

Dreaming in seed of Love's ancestral rose,

To meadows where a braver north-wind blows
O'er greener grass, o'er hedge-rose, may,
and broom,
And all that make East England's field-
perfume
Dearer than any fragrance Persia knows.

Hear us, ye winds, North, East, and West and
South,
This granite covers him whose golden mouth
Made wiser ev'n the Word of Wisdom's
King:
Blow softly over Omar's Western herald
Till roses rich of Omar's dust shall spring
From richer dust of Suffolk's rare Fitzgerald.

QUEEN KATHERINE

ON SEEING MISS ELLEN TERRY AS KATHERINE
IN "KING HENRY VIII."

SEEKING a tongue for tongueless shadow-land,

    Has Katherine's soul come back with power

        to quell

    A sister-soul incarnate, and compel

Its bodily voice to speak by Grief's command ?

Or is it Katherine's self returns to stand

    As erst she stood defying Wolsey's spell—

    Returns with those wild wrongs she fain

        would tell

Which Memory bore to Eden's amaranth-

        strand ?

Or is it thou, dear friend—this Queen, whose
   face
   The salt of many tears hath scarred and
      stung ?—
   Can it be thou, whose genius, ever young,
Lighting the body with the spirit's grace,
Is loved by England—loved by all the race
   Round all the world enlinked by Shake-
      speare's tongue !

DICKENS RETURNS ON CHRISTMAS DAY

A ragged girl in Drury Lane was heard to exclaim
"Dickens dead? Then will Father Christmas die
too?"—*June* 9, 1870.

"DICKENS is dead!" Beneath that grievous
    cry
  London seemed shivering in the summer
    heat;
  Strangers took up the tale like friends that
    meet:
Dickens is dead! said they, and hurried by;
Street children stopped their games — they
    knew not why,
  But some new night seemed darkening down
    the street.

A girl in rags, staying her way-worn feet,

Cried, "Dickens dead? Will Father Christmas

    die?"

City he loved, take courage on thy way!

    He loves thee still, in all thy joys and fears.

Though he whose smile made bright thine eyes

    of grey—

    Though he whose voice, uttering thy bur-

    thened years,

    Made laughters bubble through thy sea of

    tears—

Is gone, Dickens returns on Christmas Day!

THE CHRISTMAS TREE AT "THE PINES"

LIFE still hath one romance that naught can
bury—
Not Time himself, who coffins Life's
romances—
For still will Christmas gild the year's mis-
chances,
If Childhood comes, as here, to make him
merry—
To kiss with lips more ruddy than the cherry—
To smile with eyes outshining by their glances
The Christmas tree—to dance with fairy
dances
And crown his hoary brow with leaf and berry.

N

And as to us, dear friend, the carols sung

    Are fresh as ever.   Bright is yonder bough

Of mistletoe as that which shone and swung

    When you and I and Friendship made a
        vow

    That Childhood's Christmas still should seal
        each brow—

Friendship's, and yours, and mine—and keep
        us young.

PROPHETIC PICTURES AT VENICE

I

THE WALTZ AT THE VENETIAN REVELS,
NEW YEAR'S EVE, 1866

Has she forgotten for such halls as these

    The domes the angels built in holy times,

    When wings were ours in childhood's flowery

        climes

To dance with butterflies and golden bees ?—

Forgotten how the sunny-fingered breeze

    Shook out those English harebells' magic

        chimes

    On that child-wedding morn, 'neath English

        limes,

'Mid wild-flowers tall enough to kiss her

        knees?

The love that childhood cradled—girlhood
    nursed—

  Has she forgotten it for this dull play,

  Where far-off pigmies seem to waltz and
    sway

Like dancers in a telescope reversed?

  Or does not pallid Conscience come and
    say,

"Who sells her glory of beauty stands
    accursed"?

But was it *this* that bought her—this poor
    splendour

  That won her from her troth and wild-
    flower wreath

  Who "cracked the foxglove bells" on Gray-
    land Heath,

Or played with playful winds that tried to
    bend her,

Or, tripping through the deer-park, tall and
    slender,
    Answered the larks above, the crakes be-
        neath,
    Or mocked, with glitter of laughing lips and
        teeth,
When Love grew grave—to hide her soul's
    surrender ?
Her soul's surrender! Well — yon future
    spouse
    Paid nothing for the soul! He bought, as
        rake,
    "A woman's points": kisses these lips that
        shake
The heart with wonder when they seal their
    vows—
    These eyes where hues of sky and ocean take
All shapes of love—these brows!—my darling's
    brows !

The body knows me as I touch her waist—

    The fingers throbbing through the little
        glove—

The fingers trembling at my arm above—

The breast whose pearls are heaving inter-
        laced :

All know these arms of mine that once em-
        braced.

    Though I could give no palace — only
        love—

    That gift which "only a child had dared ap-
        prove "—

The soul's sweet temple holds me uneffaced :

The body feels me " crack" those foxglove bells

    In this soft hand to "make the elfin
        thunder " :

In these pink ears I think the music swells

    To Fate's world-waltz that holds the stars
        asunder :

But 'tis the soul has learnt what Mammon
sells:

As here we spin, what are its thoughts? I
wonder.

II

THE TEMPTATION

THE SLEEPLESS NIGHT AFTER THE WALTZ AT
THE VENETIAN REVELS

WHEN hope lies dead—ah, when 'tis death to
live,

And wrongs remembered make the heart
still bleed,

Better are Sleep's kind lies for Life's blind
need

Than truth, if lies a little peace can give.

A little peace! 'tis thy prerogative,

O Sleep! to lend it; thine to quell or feed

This love that starves—this starving soul's
    long greed,
And bid Regret, the queen of hell, forgive.
Yon moon that mocks me thro' the uncurtained
    glass
    Recalls that other night, that other moon,—
    Two English lovers on a grey lagoon,—
The voices from the lantern'd gondolas,
    The kiss, the breath, the flashing eyes, and,
    soon,
The throbbing stillness: all the heaven that
    was.

(The Lover rises from his bed and opens the window. While he looks out, a pearl necklace, to which is suspended an amulet, an antique Venetian ruby cross, is thrown in. This he takes from the floor and examines with repeated exclamations of surprise. After partly dressing himself as if to go out, he suddenly stops, throws off his clothes, shuts the window, hangs the necklace and cross on the antique window-fastening; then returns to his bed and lies watching the moonlight playing round the rubies.)

III

PROPHETIC PICTURES ON THE WALLS

How red the light of New Year's morning falls
   On each emblazoned pane whose tints illume
   With prophecies the pictures round the
     room !
The warriors, doges, nobles, cardinals,
Battles, processions, floating festivals,
   Venetian girls, Venetian dames a-bloom
   With mid-life's chilly joys of gem and plume,—
All leap to life upon the kindled walls.
Each painted vision seems a living part
   Of Memory's pageant marshalled by my
     grief.
   It says, " The New Year garners no relief,
No solace for that anguish at thy heart."
   The light that falls thro' yonder amulet
   Makes every picture say, " Forget, forget."

IV

PROPHECY OF THE FIRST PICTURE

(The light falls through the rubies on the picture of "The Dark Knight and the Ferryman." The Lover reads aloud the descriptive verses on the frame.)

THE boatman sate with brawny arms em-
  browned,
  Steadying the wherry as it rocked afloat;
  The "Dark Knight" came, and on his shield
  and coat
Symbols of doom and hell's devices frowned.

He leapt aboard. "Wilt row to Devil's
  Ground
  For gold?" The man sate dumb with chok-
  ing throat.
  "Who finds the devil in his ferry-boat
Must row him," said his soul, "across the
  sound."*

---

* "He who takes the devil in his boat must row across
the sound."—OLD PROVERB.

To Devil's Ground he rowed, a sulphurous
  coast ;
  "Alight," said then the Knight, "'tis here
    we dwell."
"Nay, Dark Knight, nay, though here my
    boat hath crossed,
  I asked thee not aboard." "Thou rowest
    well ;
Who ships the devil is not always lost,
  But lost is he who rows him home to Hell."

V

PROPHECY OF THE SECOND PICTURE

*(The light falls through the rubies on the picture of
"The Damsel of the Plain." The Lover reads
aloud the descriptive verses on the frame.)*

CHILDE ROWLAND found a Damsel on the
  Plain,
  Her daffodil crown lit all her shining head ;

He kissed her mouth, and through the world
  they sped,
The beauteous, smiling world, in sun and
  rain.
But when long joys made love a golden
  chain,
  He slew her by the sea ; then, as he fled,
  Voices of earth and air and ocean said,
"The maid was Truth : God bids you meet
  again."

Between the devil and a wild, deep sea
  He met a foe more soul-compelling still ;
A feathered snake the monster seemed to be,
  And wore a wreath o' the yellow daffodil.
Then spake the devil : " Rowland, fly to me :
  When murdered Truth returns she comes to
  kill."

VI

PROPHECY OF THE THIRD PICTURE

*(The light falls through the rubies on the Rosicrucian
panel-picture called "The Rosy Scar," depicting
Christian galley-slaves on board an Algerine galley
watching, on Christmas-eve, for the promised
appearance of Rosenkreutz as a "rosy-phantom."
The Lover reads aloud the descriptive verses on the
frame.)*

"While Night's dark horses waited for the
wind,

He stood—he shone—where Sunset's fiery
glaives

Flickered behind the clouds; then, o'er the
waves,

He came to them, Faith's remnant sorrow-
thinned.

The Paynim sailors clustering, tawny-skinned,

Cried, 'Who, is he that comes to Christian
slaves?

Nor water-sprite nor jinni of sunset caves,

The rosy phantom stands nor winged nor
    finned."

All night he stood till shone the Christmas-
    star;

  Slowly the Rosy Cross, streak after streak,

Flushed the grey sky—flushed sea and sail
    and spar,

    Flushed, blessing every slave's woe-wasted
    cheek.

    Then did great Rosenkreutz, the Dew-King,
    speak:

"Sufferers, take heart, Christ lends the Rosy
    Scar."

    *   *   *   *   *

    *   *   *   *   o

VII

NEW YEAR'S MORNING, 1867, AT VENICE
AFTER HER LIBERATION

*(The Lover goes to the window and gazes down the Grand
Canal, over which the morning is glowing.)*

" Man's knowledge, save before his fellow
man,

Is ignorance—his widest wisdom folly.

In Nature's eyes still gazing, dazzled wholly

By sights his own eyes make, how should he
scan

Pictures like those in Nature's iris-span?

Hers show the cypress, his the melancholy,

His shine with Christmas, hers with simple
holly

That knew no mirth till Yule-tide feasts began."

So Reason says; yet to my heart it seems

That yonder sun, firing the mists of
morn,

Gilding each dome that scorned the Austrian's
  scorn,

Painting the Grand Canal with rosy gleams,

Looks conscious down on me and vanished
  dreams—

  But — Freedom's year o'er Venice smiles
  new-born !

WHAT THE SILENT VOICES SAID

A SONNET SEQUENCE

I

IN WESTMINSTER ABBEY

"As the procession wound through the vast
fane, bars and curiously formed flakes of golden
light would, every now and then, break through
the gloomy atmosphere and play along the tops
of the arches and the roof."

"Love is the spirit's life and withers never:

  We twain shall meet again on some bright

    shore!"

So spake my heart, but still within its core

Whisper'd that foe who mocks the soul's en-

    deavour:

" The very greatness of the man shall sever

o

Thy soul from such a soul so wing'd to
　　soar:
Love wins no starry strand that can restore
To thee a soul whose pinions mount for ever."

Though well I knew the voice was coward
　　Fear's,
It marred the solemn music in mine ears,
　Till, sudden, through the vapour-curtain grey
Veiling the roof, fluttered a flake of light:
　A golden hand it seemed: I saw it play
Along the roof—along the "Lantern's" height.

II

THE GOLDEN HAND

Was it a sign from those, forgot by Fame,
　Who built the minster—built by that same
　　spell

Which bids the honey-bee fit cell to cell—

Who shaped in joy until dead stone became

A thing of life—who worked with poet's aim

When seized by song to make what shall
compel

The maker's own fierce heart to say " 'Tis
well "—

Careless for other praise, for other blame ?

For I recalled how scarce three years before

I followed Browning down the sacred floor,

When minster-spirits seemed to haunt the
fane :—

Heroes of song and those whose blood was
spilt

For England and those nameless ones who
built

Our temple seemed to join the funeral
train.

III

THE GOLDEN SCROLL

"THAT beckoning hand," I said, " mysterious,
  golden,
    Playing along the roof in bright unrest
    As if in welcome of this royal guest :
Comes it from those who built these arches
  olden ? "
But as I spoke it changed : a scroll unfolden
    Shone with the master's words that oft had
      bless'd
    My heart in youth when, dark and sorely
      press'd,
It yearned for light to strengthen and em-
  bolden.

I read the words that helped me when a boy
    Roaming with book in hand the Ouse's side :

I drew again, from founts that cannot cloy,

    Draughts of immortal song, till Faith defied

Fear's hissing head, and poetry and joy

    And youth returned, and grief was quelled

        by pride.

IV

THE MINSTER SPIRITS

" BEHOLD, ye builders, demigods who made

    England's Walhalla, ye who haunt this pile

    Of living stone ! behold us here defile

Behind this pall, winding through light and

        shade

Of arch and pillar, where such bones are laid

    As Time can only breed in one loved isle—

    'Tis Tennyson we bring : he was erewhile

Our king," I said ; " we loved him undis-

        mayed ! "

Sorrow had fled ; for pride and joy of him
    Made Life seem Death—made Death seem
        Life's own life—
    And more and more the mighty fane grew
        rife
With spirits mighty.   Yet mine eyes grew dim
    For her who watch'd at Aldworth, that dear
        wife
He loved so well, when rose her loving hymn.

V

THE SILENT VOICES

SWEET was the sweet wife's music, and
        consoling :
    The past returned : I heard the master's talk,
    That many a time in many a happy walk
I heard when through the whin of Aldworth
        strolling,

Or on the cliffs of Wight with billows rolling
    Below the jaggy walls of gleaming chalk :
    Again I saw him stay his giant-stalk
To watch the foamy-crested breakers shoaling.

And when the music ceased and pictures fled
    I walked as in a dream around the grave,
And looked adown and saw the flowers out-
        spread,
    And spirit-voices spake from aisle and nave:—
    " To follow him be true, be pure, be brave :
Thou needest not his lyre," the voices said.

VI

WHAT THE VOICES SAID

" BEYOND the sun, beyond the furthest star,
    Shines still the land which poets still may win
    Whose poems are their lives—whose souls
        within

Hold naught in dread save Art's high
    conscience-bar—
Who have for muse a maiden free from scar—
    Who know how beauty dies at touch of
        sin—
    Who love mankind, yet, having gods for kin,
    Breathe zephyrs, in the street, from climes
        afar.

Heedless of phantom Fame—heedless of all
    Save pity and love to light the life of
        Man—
    True poets work, winning a sunnier span
For Nature's martyr—Night's ancestral thrall:
True poets work, yet listen for the call
    Bidding them join their country and their
        clan."

OCTOBER 1892

I SEE thee pine like her in golden story

 Who, in her prison, woke and saw, one

  day,

 The gates thrown open—saw the sunbeams

  play,

With only a web 'tween her and summer's

  glory;

Who, when that web—so frail, so transitory,

 It broke before her breath—had fallen

  away,

 Saw other webs and others rise for aye

Which kept her prisoned till her hair was

  hoary.

Those songs half-sung that yet were all
    divine—

  That woke Romance, the queen, to reign
    afresh—

Had been but preludes from that lyre of thine,

  Could thy rare spirit's wings have pierced
    the mesh

  Spun by the wizard who compels the flesh,

But lets the poet see how heav'n can shine.

CHRISTINA ROSSETTI

THE TWO CHRISTMASTIDES

I

On Winter's woof, which scarcely seems of
    snow,
  But hangs translucent, like a virgin's veil,
  O'er headstone, monument, and guardian-
    rail,
The New Year's sun shines golden—seems to
    throw
Upon her coffin-flowers a greeting glow
  From lands she loved to think on—seems to
    trail
  Love's holy radiance from the very Grail
O'er those white flowers before they sink below.

Is that a spirit or bird whose sudden song
　　From yonder sunlit tree beside the grave
Recalls a robin's warble, sweet yet strong,
　　Upon a lawn beloved of wind and wave—
　　Recalls her "Christmas Robin," ruddy,
　　　　brave,
Winning the crumbs she throws where black-
　　　　birds throng?

II

In Christmastide of heaven does *she* recall
　　Those happy days with Gabriel by the
　　　　sea,
　　Who gathered round him those he loved,
　　　　when she
"Must coax the birds to join the festival,"
And said, "The sea-sweet winds are musical
　　With carols from the billows singing free

Around the groynes, and every shrub and
    tree
Seems conscious of the Channel's rise and
    fall " ?

The coffin lowers, and I can see her now—
    See the loved kindred standing by her side,
As once I saw them 'neath our Christmas
    bough—
    And her, that dearer one, who sanctified
    With halo of mother's love our Christmas-
    tide—
And Gabriel too—with peace upon his brow.

TO A SLEEPER AT ROME

For the unveiling by Edmund Gosse of the
American memorial bust to the poet Keats in
Hampstead Parish Church, July 16, 1894.

THY gardens, bright with limbs of gods at
    play—
  Those bowers whose flowers are fruits,
    Hesperian sweets
  That light with heaven the soul of him who
    eats,
And lend his veins Olympian blood of day—
Were only lent, and, since thou couldst not
    stay,
  Better to die than wake in sorrow, Keats,

Where even the Siren's song no longer
　　cheats—
Where Love's long "Street of Tombs" still
　　lengthens grey.

Better to nestle there in arms of Flora,
　　Ere Youth—the king of Earth and Beauty's
　　　heir,
Drinking such breath in meadows of Aurora
　　As bards of morning drank, Ægean air—
Wake in old age's caverns of Ellora,
　　Carven with visions dead and sights that
　　　were!

IN A GRAVEYARD

OLIVER MADOX BROWN

NOVEMBER 12, 1874

FAREWELL to thee, and to our dreams fare-
well—
  Dreams of high deeds and golden days of
  thine,
  Where once again should Art's twin powers
  combine—
The painter's wizard-wand, the poet's spell!
Though Death strikes free, careless of Heaven
  and Hell—
  Careless of Man, of Love's most lovely shrine;
  Yet must Man speak—must ask of Heaven a
  sign
That this wild world is God's, and all is well.

Last night we mourned thee, cursing eyeless
    Death,
Who, sparing sons of Baal and Ashtoreth,
    Must needs slay thee, with all the world to
        slay;
    But round this grave the winds of winter say:
"On earth what hath the poet? An alien
        breath.
    Night holds the keys that ope the doors of
        Day."

TWO LETTERS TO A FRIEND

LETTER I.

AFTER THE WEDDING

BRIGHT-BROWED as Summer's self, who claspt
    the land,
  With eyes like English skies, where seemed
    to play
Deep azure dreams behind the tender grey,
All light and love, she moved: I see her stand
Beneath that tree; I see the happy band
  Of bridesmaids on the lawn where blossoms
    sway
  In light so rare, it seems as if the day
Glowed   conscious   of   the   future's   rosy
    strand.

O Friend, if sun and wind and flowers and
    birds,
In language deeper drawn than human words,
From deeper founts than Time shall e'er
    destroy,
    All spoke to thee in Summer's rich caress,
    Even so my heart, though wordless too,
      could bless ;
It could but feel a joy to know thy joy.

LETTER II.

AFTER DEATH'S MOCKERY

WHEN death from out the dark, by one blind
    blow,
    Strikes down Love's heart of hearts—severs
      a life—
Cleaves it in twain as by a sudden knife,
Leaving the dreadful Present, dumb with woe,

Mocked by a Past, whose rainbow-skies aglow

O'erarch Love's bowers, where all his flowers

seem rife

In bloom of one sweet loving girl and wife—

Then Friendship's voice must whisper, whisper

low.

Though well I know 'tis thou who dost inherit

Heroic blood and faith that lends the spirit

Strength known to souls like thine, of noblest

strain,

Comfort I dare not proffer.   What relief

Shall Friendship proffer Love in such wild

grief?

I can but suffer pain to know thy pain:

I can but suffer pain; and yet to me

Returns that day whose light seemed heavenly

light,

Whose breath seemed incense rising to unite

That lawn—where every flower and bird and

    bee

Seemed loving her who shone beneath that

    tree—

    With lawns far off, whose flowers of higher

       delight,

    Beyond Death's icy peaks and fens of night,

Bloomed 'neath a heaven her eyes, not ours,

    could see.

Brother, did Nature mock us with that glory

Which seemed to prophesy Love's rounded

    story ?

    Or was it that sweet Summer's fond device

To show thee who shall stand on Eden slopes,

Where bloom the broken buds of earthly

    hopes—

    Stand waiting 'neath a tree of Paradise ?

ANCESTRAL MEMORY

THE DEAF AND DUMB SON OF CRŒSUS

HE saw their spears who scaled the parapet,
  Then—pouring, glittering, with a torrent's
    force,
  Through battered gates—the spears! With-
    out remorse
He struck, he slew, round Crœsus sore beset.
He heard not Slaughter's din, but felt her
    sweat
  And smelt her breath where many a bloody
    corse,
  Trampled by Persian camel, Lydian horse,
Showed how at Sardis Fate and Crœsus met.

But when he saw his father down at last—

    Down, waiting death at some fierce foeman's

        stroke—

Louder the dumb boy shrieked than Winter's

        blast :

    " Man, kill not Crœsus ! "

                'Twas the Race that spoke :

The blood of Lydian Kings within him woke

Ancestral memory—woke the sceptred Past.

APOLLO IN PARIS

TO THE FRENCH ACADEMY ON THE ELECTION
OF M. J. M. DE HÉRÉDIA

I

SPIRES, roofs, and towers gleam in the sunset's
glow
Till Paris burns like some old poet-town
That draws Apollo's radiant presence down
By music mounting from his sons below:
Methinks he greets you, fearless men who know
His sons and guard them, lest their sire's
renown
Be dimmed when bastard fingers clutch the
crown
Of him, our Lord of light and lyre and bow.

As when he scared the hordes who sacked old
>Rome

That day he soared above his temple-dome
>When gods were fleeing the voices of the
>Vandals,

I see him now whose song keeps heaven
>immortal ;

I see him now : he shines above your portal,
>Phœbus from golden curls to golden
>sandals !

II

With limbs of light I see the song-god stand
>Flushing your roof ! He knows your hands
>are strong

Against his foes, the brazen-throated throng,
Whose breath is blight to beauty in every
>land ;

" Foes of my foes," saith he, " who dare with-
 stand
 The great coarse voice that works my
 children wrong,
 Ye crown Hérédia with the crown of song
Heedless of all save Art's divine command !

He sings the past—the beauty that hath been :
 I love him, I—remembering those bright
 days
 Before the world grew grey of Vandal haze,
When gods might mix with men of godlike
 mien
And maids with lovesome eyes of mortal
 sheen,
 Sweet goddesses of earth with Woman's
 ways :

III

I love the song-born poet, for that he

    Loves only song—seeks for love's sake alone

    Shy Poesie, whose dearest bowers, unknown

To feudaries of Fame, are known to me."

So saith the god, in tones which seem to be

    That music of the sunset richly blown

      When sinks the sun-god from his sinking

        throne

Within the burnished bosom of the sea.

He soars away, a star in rosy air;

But see ! the memory of his presence there

    Lives where he stood. Yea, though a god

      hath fled,

Leaving a fading memory scarce beholden,

A true god's very shadow glimmers golden

    With lovelier light than mortal brows can

      shed.

ENVOY.

The poet sings what Nature, dreaming, saith,

But still his Bride is Art—that starry
wife

From shores where music of the gods is
rife.

She teaches him the strain that conquereth,

Whether he touch the lyre, or breathe his
breath

Through flute of Phœbus or through Pan's
wild fife—

Whether of Man he sings or Nature's life,

Or shining sward beyond the dykes of death.

Yet, though he asks but this, the Bride's
acclaim—

Though not Fame's trumpet nor the wreath of
Fame

Can give the bridegroom joy whose Bride is
    Art—

He grieves when bastard-brows are crowned
    with flowers,

And Helicon grows noisier than a mart—

Remembering Poesie within her bowers.

AT THE THÉATRE FRANÇAIS

ON THE REVIVAL, AFTER FIFTY YEARS, OF "LE
ROI S'AMUSE"

NOVEMBER 22, 1882

POET of pity and scourge of sceptred crime—
  Titan of light, with scarce the gods for
    peers—
  What thoughts come to thee through the
    mist of years,
There sitting calm, master of Fate and Time ?
Homage from every tongue, from every
    clime,
  In place of gibes, fills now thy satiate ears.
  Mine own heart swells, mine eyelids prick
    with tears

In very pride of thee, old man sublime !

And thou, the mother who bore him, beauteous
    France,
    Round whose fair limbs what web of sorrow
      is spun !—

I see thee lift thy tear-stained countenance—
    Victress by many a victory he hath won ;

I hear thy voice o'er winds of Fate and Chance
    Say to the conquered world: " Behold my
      son ! "

TO MADAME CARNOT *

At Dijon gleamed on that bright coun-
    tenance—
Illumed by love of thee and love of those
Who sprang from thee—tears born of
    coming woes.
The sad prophetic Spirit of joyous France
Wept too, methinks, to see her son advance

* "When the President reached Dijon he had the
happiness to find awaiting him on the railway platform
his son, the lieutenant, and his daughter and son-in-law,
with their little daughter, a sweet child of four. The
grandfather took her into his carriage, and embraced her
affectionately, and said how much more pleasant it would
be to get out and stay at Dijon with her than to go on to
Lyons. His eyes filled with tears as he gave her the
parting kiss, and handed her to her father."—DAILY NEWS,
June 25, 1894.

To death ; and when he kissed the child
there rose

That sight the Future's mirror sometimes
shows,

The mother-land in grip of Fate or Chance.

" Daughter," saith France to thee, " this day of
sorrow

Wins for his threatened land a sunnier
morrow :

His was the death could save me—not
another :

For me thy dear one robbed thee of his life—

For me fought, bosom bare—yea, met the knife

Hell whetted for the bosom of his Mother."

THE LAST WALK FROM BOAR'S HILL

TO A. C. S.

I

ONE after one they go; and glade and heath,
  Where once we walked with them, and
    garden-bowers
  They made so dear, are haunted by the
    hours
Once musical of those who sleep beneath;
One after one does Sorrow's every wreath
  Bind closer you and me with funeral flowers,
  And Love and Memory from each loss of
    ours
Forge conquering glaives to quell the conqueror
  Death.

Since Love and Memory now refuse to yield

The friend with whom we walk through mead
    and field

  To-day as on that day when last we parted,

Can he be dead, indeed, whatever seem ?

Love shapes a presence out of Memory's
    dream,

  A living presence, Jowett golden-hearted.

II

Can he be dead ?   We walk through flowery
    ways

  From Boar's Hill down to Oxford, fain to
    know

  What nugget-gold, in drift of Time's long
    flow,

The Bodleian mine hath stored from richer
    days ;

He, fresh as on that morn, with sparkling
    gaze,
  Hair bright as sunshine, white as moonlit
    snow,
  Still talks of Plato while the scene below
Breaks gleaming through the veil of sunlit
    haze.

Can he be dead ? He shares our homeward
    walk,
And by the river you arrest the talk
  To see the sun transfigure ere he sets
The boatmen's children shining in the wherry
  And on the floating bridge the ply-rope
    wets,
Making the clumsy craft an angel's ferry.

III

The river crossed, we walk 'neath glowing
   skies

   Through grass where cattle feed or stand
      and stare

   With burnished coats, glassing the coloured
      air—

Fading as colour after colour dies :

We pass the copse ; we round the leafy
      rise—

   Start many a coney and partridge, hern and
      hare ;

   We win the scholar's nest—his simple fare

Made royal-rich by welcome in his eyes.

Can he be dead ?   His heart was drawn to
      you.

Ah ! well that kindred heart within him
      knew

The poet's heart of gold that gives the spell!

Can he be dead?   Your heart being drawn to
    him,

How shall ev'n Death make that dear presence
    dim

  For you who loved him—us who loved him
    well?

THE OCTOPUS OF THE GOLDEN ISLES

"What! Will they even strike at me?"

ROUND many an Isle of Song, in seas serene,
  With many a swimmer strove the poet-boy,
  Yet strove in love: their strength, I say, was joy
To him, my friend—dear friend of godlike mien!
But soon he felt beneath the billowy green
  A monster moving—moving to destroy:
  Limb after limb became the tortured toy
Of coils that clung and lips that stung unseen.

" *And canst thou strike ev'n me ?* " the swimmer
said,
As rose above the waves the deadly eyes,
Arms flecked with mouths that kissed in
hellish wise,
Quivering in hate around a hateful head.—
I saw him fight old Envy's sorceries:
I saw him sink: the man I loved is dead!

LOVE HOLDS OF HEAVEN IN FEE

AT A FUNERAL

I

THESE tears, as down the slope Death's pageant
   wends—
   These tears, whence come they—tears I
      cannot smother?
Is it for thee they flow, my brother's brother?
Is it for him they flow, or these dear friends?
My thoughts are far away where water bends
   Around a grange—my thoughts are with
      that other
   Who held thee—yea, ere thou couldst babble
      " Mother,"
Who holds thee still by strength that never
   ends.

She holds thee—she who, like the mother-
    dove,
  Draws near her nestlings only to caress,
Whose love for thee, for them, boundless,
    above
  All other wealth of Woman's tenderness,
    Is not their dower alone : its boon can bless
All eyes which see that mother's eyes of love.

II

She holds thee still : Love holds of heaven in
    fee :
  Still lives that face where Nature seemed to
    write
  Life's twin-ancestral story in mingled light
On lips whose smile was hers of love or glee,
In eyes whose pictures from the blue-grey sea,
  Radiant of laughters, radiant in despite

Of shadowy bars from lashes dark as night,
Seemed like a sailor's memory haunting thee.

She holds thee still; Death dares not dim that
    face
Rich with the runes of each historic race,
    Where, like the message of an olden scroll
Deep-glimmering in a priceless palimpsest,
The language of the past seemed half-exprest
    Beneath the scriptures of a new-lit soul.

THE WOOD-HAUNTER'S DREAM

THE wild things loved me, but a wood-sprite
  said :
  "Though meads are sweet when flowers at
    morn uncurl,
  And woods are sweet with nightingale and
    merle,
Where are the dreams that flush'd thy childish
  bed ?
The Spirit of the Rainbow thou wouldst wed!"
  I rose, I found her—found a rain-drench'd
    girl
  Whose eyes of azure and limbs like roseate
    pearl
Coloured the rain above her golden head.

But when I stood by that sweet vision's side

    I saw no more the Rainbow's lovely stains;

To her by whom the glowing heavens were

        dyed

    The sun showed naught but dripping woods

        and plains :

    "God gives the world the Rainbow, her the

        rains,"

The wood-sprite laugh'd, " our seeker finds a

        bride."

MIDSHIPMAN LANYON

"Midshipman Lanyon refused to leave the
Admiral and perished."—TIMES, *June* 30, 1893.

OUR tears are tears of pride who see thee
stand,
  Watching the great bows dip, the stern
  uprear,
  Beside thy chief, whose hope was still to
  steer,
Though Fate had said, "Ye shall not win the
land!"
What joy was thine to answer each command
  From him calamity had made more dear,
  Save that which bade thee part when Death
  drew near,
Till Tryon sank with Lanyon at his hand!

Death only and doom are sure: they come,
    they rend,
    But still the fight we make can crown us
      great:
    Life hath no joy like his who fights with
      Fate
Shoulder to shoulder with a stricken friend:
    Proud are our tears for thee, most fortunate,
Whose day, so brief, had such heroic end.

A REMINISCENCE OF THE OPEN-AIR PLAYS *

TO PIERROT IN LOVE

THE CLOWN WHOSE KISSES TURNED A CRONE
TO A FAIRY-QUEEN

WHAT dost thou here, in Love's enchanted wood,

    Pierrot, who once wert safe as clown and

        thief—

Held safe by love of fun and wine and food—

    From her who follows love of Woman,

        Grief—

* Epilogue for the open-air performance of Banville's
" Le Baiser," in which Lady Archibald Campbell took the
part of " Pierrot " and Miss Annie Schletter the part of
the " Fairy."—COOMBE, *August* 9, 1889.

Her who, of old, stalked over Eden-grass

   Behind Love's baby-feet—whose shadow

      threw

On every brook, as on a magic glass,

Prophetic shapes of what should come to pass

   When tears got mixt with Paradisal dew?

Kisses are loved but for the lips that kiss:

   Thine have restored a princess to her throne,

Breaking the spell which barred from fairy

      bliss

   A fay and shrank her to a wrinkled crone;

But, if thou dream'st that thou from Pantomime

   Shalt clasp an angel of the mystic moon—

Clasp her on banks of Love's own rose and

      thyme,

While woodland warblers ring the nuptial-

      chime—

   Bottom to thee were but a meek buffoon.

                  R

When yonder fairy, long ago, was told
   The spell which caught her in malign eclipse,
Turning her radiant body foul and old,
    Would yield to some knight-errant's virgin
       lips,
And when, through many a weary day and
       night,
   She, wondering who the paladin would be
Whose kiss should charm her from her grievous
       plight,
Pictured a-many princely heroes bright,
   Dost thou suppose she ever pictured thee ?

'Tis true the mischief of the foeman's charm
   Yielded to thee—to that first kiss of thine.
We saw her tremble—lift a rose-wreath arm,
   Which late, all veined and shrivelled, made
      her pine ;
We saw her fingers rise and touch her cheek,

As if the morning breeze across the wood,
  Which lately seemed to strike so chill and
    bleak
Through all the wasted body, bent and weak,
  Were light and music now within her blood.

'Tis true thy kiss made all her form expand—
  Made all the skin grow smooth and pure as
    pearl,
Till there she stood, tender, yet tall and
    grand,
  A queen of Faëry yet a lovesome girl,
Within whose eyes—whose wide, new-litten
    eyes—
  New litten by thy kiss's re-creation—
Expectant joy that yet was wild surprise
Made all her flesh like light of summer skies
  When dawn lies dreaming of the morn's
    carnation.

But when thou saw'st the breaking of the spell
  Within whose grip of might her soul had
      pined,
Like some sweet butterfly that breaks the cell
  In which its purple pinions slept confined,
And when thou heard'st the strains of elfin song
  Her sisters sang from rainbow cars above
      her—
Didst thou suppose that she, though prisoned
      long,
And freed at last by thee from all the wrong,
  Must for that kiss take Harlequin for lover?

Hearken, sweet fool! Though Banville carried
      thee
  To lawns where love and song still share
      the sward
Beyond the golden river few can see
  And fewer still, in these grey days, can ford;

And though he bade the wings of Passion fan

  Thy face, till every line grows bright and

    human,

Feathered thy spirit's wing for wider span,

And fired thee with the fire that comes to man

  When first he plucks the rose of Nature,

    Woman;

And though our actress gives thee that sweet

    gaze

  Where spirit and matter mingle in liquid

    blue—

That face, where pity through the frolic

    plays—

  That form, whose lines of light Love's pencil

    drew—

That voice, whose music seems a new caress

  Whenever passion makes a new transition

From key to key of joy or quaint distress—

That sigh, when, now, thy fairy's loveliness
  Leaves thee alone to mourn Love's vanished
    vision :

Still art thou Pierrot—naught but Pierrot ever ;
  For is not this the very word of Fate :
" No mortal, clown or king, shall e'er dissever
  His present glory from his past estate " ?
Yet be thou wise and dry those foolish tears ;
  The clown's first kiss was needed, not the
    clown,
By her who, fired by hopes and chilled by fears,
Sought but a kiss like thine for years on years :
  Be wise, I say, and wander back to town.

LECONTE DE LISLE

July 17, 1894

A REMINISCENCE OF THE JUBILEE REVIVAL
OF " LE ROI S'AMUSE " November 22, 1882

Where'er thou art, canst thou forget that night
   When, after fifty years, the victory came,
      And Hugo—throned above all thrones of
         Fame—
Watched his own mighty dream uncoil its
         might,
And thou didst stand with shining locks of white
   And eyes that, answering our proud hearts'
      acclaim,
   Lost all their arrowy mockeries, and became
Dim with the tears that made their lashes
      bright ?

Nirvana was thy quest !   But love like thine

    For that great soul must bear thy kindled

       soul

Where Love's high-chosen constellations shine

    Of stars unmingled with the " loveless

       Whole " :

When love hath coloured life with hues divine,

    What poet secks Nirvana's hueless goal ?

TO BRITAIN AND AMERICA

ON THE DEATH OF JAMES RUSSELL LOWELL

YE twain who long forgot your brotherhood
  And those far fountains whence, through
    glorious years,
  Your fathers drew, for Freedom's pioneers,
Your English speech, your dower of English
    blood—
Ye ask to-day, in sorrow's holiest mood,
  When all save love seems film—ye ask in
    tears—
  "How shall we honour him whose name
    endears
The footprints where belovèd Lowell stood?"

Your hands he joined—those fratricidal hands,
　　Once trembling, each, to seize a brother's
　　　　throat :
How shall ye honour him whose spirit stands
　　Between you still ?—Keep Love's bright
　　　　sails afloat,
　　For Lowell's sake, where once ye strove and
　　　　smote
On waves that must unite, not part, your
　　strands.

TO MRS. GARFIELD

Such strength as his, striving in such a strife,
  Will win at last: God gave thy dear one
    all:
A seat above the conflict, power to call
Peace like a Zephyr, when alarms were rife;
Home music too, children and heroine wife,
  God gave: then gave Death's writing on the
    wall,
  And on the road the assassin: bade him
    fall,
Death-stricken at the shining crest of Life.

And yet our tears are sweet.   God bade him
    taste
  All gifts of heav'n, like manna raining
    down—
  Clothed him with Good for Might, whose
    sweet renown
Touched Ocean's lyre to music as it passed;
Then crowned him thine indeed—giving at last
  Pain suffered well,—thy Garfield's deathless
    crown.

Sixteenth Edition.   In One Volume.   Crown 8vo, gilt top.   Price 6s.

AYLWIN

By THEODORE WATTS-DUNTON

Author of

"The Coming of Love: Rhona Boswell's Story"

SOME PRESS OPINIONS

"The appearance of a novel from the hand of a poet and critic is an interesting event. The interest of Mr Watts-Dunton's 'Aylwin' is heightened also by the fact that the author is known to have drawn largely on his reminiscences for his material—to have mingled *Wahrheit* and *Dichtung*. The reader, therefore, expects, and will not fail to find himself in the company of some of the most remarkable men of genius of our time."—*Times.*

"The author of 'Aylwin' has a certain kinship with the creator of Wilhelm Meister."—*Literary World.*

"A fascinating book, the outcome of real art, the reflex of a real personality. The mere writing of it rises at times to the very poetry of prose."—*Academy.*

"To name a finer love story than this would tax the best-stored memory."—*World.*

"Full of the open air, full of passion, with a skilfully contrived plot, which hurries the reader on breathless from page to page."—Dr ROBERTSON NICOLL in the *Sketch.*

"Un récit très poétique, fort bien conduit. M. Dunton s'est attaché à montrer qu 'aucun homme ayant aimé une femme d'un profond amour spirituel ne saurait être matérialiste.' Cette opinion est comme le *leit-motiv* de son ouvrage. Elle este exprimée avec un rare éloquence par divers personnages, surtout par le peintre d'Arcy, en qui les lecteurs Anglais ont tout de suite reconnu un portrait de Rossetti, qui fut de son vivant l'intime ami de M. Dunton."—*Journal des Débats.*

"A vivid, enthralling, absorbing love-story, full of movement, life and vigour. Its open-air freshness, its thrilling interest, and its intense and noble passion, will make it one of the most eagerly read novels of recent years."—*Daily Chronicle.*

"The book is amazing in its variety and in its power, in the art with which it combines the mystical with the actual, the pomp of society with the humour and the pathos of the slum. Sinfi Lovell is one of the most finished studies of its type and kind in all romantic literature."—*Daily News.*

"We can recall no study of the love-passion that can compare with 'Aylwin.' It declines to be classed. It is of no school. It owns no lineage, acknowledges no tradition. Its form is new, its ethical message is new."—*The Star.*

"A poem in prose. Its style unpretentious, yet full of poetry; its wide variety of sympathy and diversity of scene—particularly its subtle study of gipsy life, its vein of personal reminiscence, and its spiritual teaching, combine to make it an addition, not only to our best works of fiction, but to our masterpieces of prose."—*Literature.*

"The words of 'Aylwin' come 'straight from the heart,' and consequently go straight to the heart."—*Athenæum.*

"Since 'Manon Lescaut' we have had no such tale of sentiment; and without doubt the sentiment of Mr Watts-Dunton is of a higher sort than that of the Abbé Prevost."—*Standard.*

"One of the wonders of 'Aylwin' is the artistic power with which the spiritual essences of wholly diverse characters are illustrated in a subtle unity, while at the same time the human narrative goes on sheer and strong."—*Sun.*

"Sinfi Lovell will probably prove one of the greatest heroines in fiction."—*Echo.*

LONDON: HURST AND BLACKETT, LIMITED

The Sequel to "Aylwin" is contained in

THE COMING OF LOVE

RHONA BOSWELL'S STORY

AND OTHER POEMS

By THEODORE WATTS-DUNTON

Crown 8vo, 5s. net.   *Fifth Edition*

"In 'The Coming of Love' (which, though published earlier, is a sequel to 'Aylwin') he has given us an unforgettable, we cannot but believe an enduring portrait; one of the few immortal women of the imagination. Rhona Boswell comes again into 'Aylwin.'" —*Literature.*

"On account of the haunting magic of 'The Coming of Love,' Rossetti intended to use one of the scenes for a picture—that depicted in a sonnet called 'The Stars in the River,' which he pronounced to be the 'most original of all the versions of the " Doppelganger" legend.'"—*Athenæum.*

"Superb writing; it has its chances for all time. Marked by the poet's strongest characteristics, his rare art of describing by successive images of strength and beauty."—*Daily News.*

"A work to which the student and the literary historian must turn with feelings of reverence for many a generation to come. 'Rhona' surely has come to stay in English poetry."—*Sun.*

"Gives the author a definite, permanent, and distinguished position among present-day poets."—*Globe.*

"Original and interesting, fresh in subject and feeling."—*The Times.*

"Has the distinctive quality of not resembling the work of any other poet."—*Pall Mall Gazette.*

"'The Coming of Love' is a striking story, powerfully told."—*Daily Chronicle.*

"Here unquestionably is the grand style which Arnold so often desiderated in modern verse. By the sonnets in the second half of his volume, Mr Watts-Dunton ranks among the foremost of living poets."—*St James' Gazette.*

"In a succession of tableaux—sometimes so vivid and realistic that we seem to be looking at a canvas rather than a printed page; at other times as cloudy and uncanny as the shadow-scenes depicted in a beryl stone or magic crystal,—Mr Watts-Dunton contrives to present before us the evolution of a soul."—*Sketch.*

JOHN LANE

THE BODLEY HEAD LONDON AND NEW YORK

" Spirited and patriotic."—*Guardian*.

" Contains some fine patriotic poetry."—*Leeds Mercury*.

" From the accomplished pen of Mr. Theodore Watts-Dunton, whose poetical work is destined before long (we believe) to receive the widespread appreciation it deserves."
Globe.

" This poem is interesting by reason of its daring attempt to throw the glamour of poetry upon modern ships of war."—*Morning Leader*.

" This noble composition . . . is necessarily something of a battle cry."—*Daily News*.

" The great Naval Review has here been made the occasion for publishing a patriotic poem of high merit by Mr. Watts-Dunton."—*Christian World*.

" Among the many poems written in honour of the Longest Reign Celebration, Mr. Theodore Watts-Dunton's ' Greeting at Spithead ' attracts the attention."
Morning Post.

" Fine verses in an exalted vein of Imperial patriotism."
St. James's Gazette.

" The whole ode is animated by a noble and virile spirit."—*British Review*.

" A splendid contribution to our treasury of patriotic poetry."—*Glasgow Herald*.

" One bard, and one only, in England has clothed in deathless song the spirit of this stirring period of Imperial triumph.   Mr. Watts-Dunton is amongst the first makers of nineteenth-century verse."—*African Critic*.

" Brother craftsmen will appreciate the skill with which phrase is built upon phrase and line upon line, each stanza being wrought powerfully to a clinching close. Here practically is a new voice in English poetry with an accent and a message of its own."—*Athenæum*.

JOHN LANE

THE BODLEY HEAD
VIGO ST
W.
Telegrams
"BODLEIAN LONDON"

E. NEW.

CATALOGUE *of* PUBLICATIONS *in* BELLES LETTRES

List of Books

IN

BELLES LETTRES

Published by John Lane

𝕿𝖍𝖊 𝕭𝖔𝖉𝖑𝖊𝖞 𝕳𝖊𝖆𝖉

VIGO STREET, LONDON, W.

Adams (Francis).
ESSAYS IN MODERNITY. Crown 8vo. 5s. net. [*Shortly.*
A CHILD OF THE AGE. Crown 8vo. 3s. 6d. net.

A. E.
HOMEWARD: SONGS BY THE WAY. Sq. 16mo, wrappers, 1s. 6d. net. (*Second Edition.*
THE EARTH BREATH, AND OTHER POEMS. Sq. 16mo. 3s. 6d. net.

Æsop's Fables.
A HUNDRED FABLES OF. With 101 Full-page Illustrations by P. J. BILLINGHURST, and an Introductory Note by KENNETH GRAHAME. Fcap. 4to. 6s.

Aldrich (T. B.).
LATER LYRICS. Sm. fcap. 8vo. 2s. 6d. net.

Allen (Grant).
THE LOWER SLOPES : A Volume of Verse. Crown 8vo. 5s. net.
THE WOMAN WHO DID. Crown 8vo. 3s. 6d. net. (*Twenty-third Edition.*
THE BRITISH BARBARIANS. Crown 8vo. 3s. 6d. net. [*Second Edition.*

Atherton (Gertrude).
PATIENCE SPARHAWK AND HER TIMES. Crown 8vo. 6s. [*Third Edition.*
THE CALIFORNIANS. Crown 8vo. 6s. [*Third Edition.*

Bailey (John C.).
ENGLISH ELEGIES. Crown 8vo. 5s. net. [*In preparation.*

Balfour (Marie Clothilde).
MARIS STELLA. Crown 8vo. 3s. 6d. net.
SONGS FROM A CORNER OF FRANCE. [*In preparation.*

Beardsley (Aubrey).
EARLY WORK OF. Edited by H. C. MARILLIER. With nearly 150 Illustrations. 4to. 21s. net. *Also a limited edition printed on Japanese vellum, at* 42s. net.

Beeching (Rev. H. C.).
IN A GARDEN : Poems. Crown 8vo. 5s. net.
ST. AUGUSTINE AT OSTIA. Crown 8vo, wrappers. 1s. net.

Beerbohm (Max).
THE WORKS OF MAX BEERBOHM. With a Bibliography by JOHN LANE. Sq. 16mo. 4s. 6d. net.
THE HAPPY HYPOCRITE. Sq. 16mo. 1s. net. [*Third Edition.*
MORE. Sq. 16mo. 4s. 6d. net.

Bell (J. J.).
THE NEW NOAH'S ARK. Illustrated in Colours. 4to. 3s. 6d.

Bennett (E. A.).
A MAN FROM THE NORTH. Crown 8vo. 3s. 6d.
JOURNALISM FOR WOMEN : A Practical Guide. Sq. 16mo. 2s. 6d. net.

Benson (Arthur Christopher).
LYRICS. Fcap. 8vo, buckram. 5s. net.
LORD VYET AND OTHER POEMS. Fcap. 8vo. 3s. 6d. net.

Bridges (Robert).
SUPPRESSED CHAPTERS AND OTHER BOOKISHNESS. Crown 8vo. 3s. 6d. net. [*Second Edition.*

Brotherton (Mary).
ROSEMARY FOR REMEMBRANCE. Fcap. 8vo. 3s. 6d. net.

Brown (Vincent)
MY BROTHER. Sq. 16mo. 2s. net.
ORDEAL BY COMPASSION. Crown 8vo. 3s. 6d.
TWO IN CAPTIVITY. Crown 8vo. 3s. 6d.
THE ROMANCE OF A RITUALIST. Crown 8vo, 6s.

Bourne (George).
A YEAR'S EXILE. Crown 8vo. 3s. 6d.

Buchan (John).
SCHOLAR GIPSIES. With 7 full-page Etchings by D. Y. CAMERON. Crown 8vo. 5s. net. [*Second Edition.*
MUSA PISCATRIX. With 6 Etchings by E. PHILIP PIMLOTT. Crown 8vo. 5s. net.
JOHN BURNET OF BARNS. A Romance. Crown 8vo. 6s.
GREY WEATHER. Crown 8vo. 6s.

Campbell (Gerald).
THE JONESES AND THE ASTERISKS. A Story in Monologue. 6 Illustrations by F. H. TOWNSEND. Fcap. 8vo. 3s. 6d. net. [*Second Edition.*

Case (Robert H.).
ENGLISH EPITHALAMIES. Crown 8vo. 5s. net.

Castle (Mrs. Egerton).
MY LITTLE LADY ANNE. Sq. 16mo. 2s. net.

Chapman (Elizabeth Rachel).
MARRIAGE QUESTIONS IN MODERN FICTION. Crown 8vo. 3s. 6d. net.

Charles (Joseph F.).
THE DUKE OF LINDEN. Crown 8vo. 3s. 6d.

Cobb (Thomas).
CARPET COURTSHIP. Crown 8vo. 3s. 6d.
MR. PASSINGHAM. Crown 8vo. 3s. 6d.

Coleridge (Ernest Hartley).
POEMS. 3s. 6d. net.

Corvo (Baron).
STORIES TOTO TOLD ME. Square 16mo. 1s. net.

Crane (Walter).
TOY BOOKS. Re-issue of.
THIS LITTLE PIG'S PICTURE BOOK, containing :
  I. THIS LITTLE PIG.
  II. THE FAIRY SHIP.
  III. KING LUCKIEBOY'S PARTY.
MOTHER HUBBARD'S PICTURE-BOOK, containing :
  IV. MOTHER HUBBARD.
  V. THE THREE BEARS.
  VI. THE ABSURD A. B. C.
CINDERELLA'S PICTURE BOOK, containing :
  VII. CINDERELLA.
  VIII. PUSS IN BOOTS.
  IX. VALENTINE AND ORSON.
RED RIDING HOOD'S PICTURE BOOK, containing :
  X. RED RIDING HOOD.
  XI. THE FORTY THIEVES.
  XII. JACK AND THE BEANSTALK.
Each Picture-Book containing three Toy Books, complete with end papers and covers, together with collective titles, end-papers, decorative cloth cover, and newly written Preface by WALTER CRANE, 4s. 6d. The Twelve Parts as above may be had separately at 1s. each.

Crackanthorpe (Hubert).
VIGNETTES. A Miniature Journal of Whim and Sentiment. Fcap. 8vo, boards. 2s. 6d. net.

Craig (R. Manifold).
THE SACRIFICE OF FOOLS. **Crown** 8vo. 6s.

Crosse (Victoria).
THE WOMAN WHO DIDN'T. **Crown** 8vo. 3s. 6d. net.
[*Third Edition.*]

Custance (Olive).
OPALS: Poems. Fcap. 8vo. 3s. 6d. net.

Croskey (Julian).
MAX. Crown 8vo. 6s.
[*Second Edition.*]

Dalmon (C. W.).
SONG FAVOURS. Sq. 16mo. 3s. 6d. net.

D'Arcy (Ella).
MONOCHROMES. Crown 8vo. 3s. 6d. net.
THE BISHOP'S DILEMMA. Crown 8vo. 3s. 6d.
MODERN INSTANCES. Crown 8vo. 3s. 6d.

Dawe (W. Carlton).
YELLOW AND WHITE. Crown 8vo. 3s. 6d. net.
KAKEMONOS. Crown 8vo. 3s. 6d. net.

Dawson (A. J.)
MERE SENTIMENT. Crown 8vo. 3s. 6d. net.
MIDDLE GREYNESS. Crown 8vo. 6s.

Davidson (John).
PLAYS: An Unhistorical Pastoral; A Romantic Farce; Bruce, a Chronicle Play; Smith, a Tragic Farce; Scaramouch in Naxos, a Pantomime. Small 4to. 7s. 6d. net.
FLEET STREET ECLOGUES. Fcap. 8vo, buckram. 4s. 6d. net.
[*Third Edition.*]
FLEET STREET ECLOGUES. 2nd Series. Fcap. 8vo, buckram. 4s. 6d. net. [*Second Edition.*]
A RANDOM ITINERARY. Fcap. 8vo. 5s. net.
BALLADS AND SONGS. Fcap. 8vo. 5s. net. [*Fourth Edition.*]
NEW BALLADS. Fcap. 8vo. 4s. 6d. net. [*Second Edition.*]
GODFRIDA. A Play Fcap. 8vo. 5s. net.

Davidson (John)—*continued.*
THE LAST BALLAD AND OTHER POEMS. Fcap. 8vo. 4s. 6d. net.

De Lyrienne (Richard).
THE QUEST OF THE GILT-EDGED GIRL. Sq. 16mo. 1s. net.

De Tabley (Lord).
POEMS, DRAMATIC AND LYRICAL. By JOHN LEICESTER WARREN (Lord de Tabley). Five Illustrations and Cover by C. S. RICKETTS. Crown 8vo. 7s. 6d net. [*Third Edition.*]
POEMS, DRAMATIC AND LYRICAL. Second Series. Crown 8vo. 5s. net.

Devereux (Roy).
THE ASCENT OF WOMAN. Crown 8vo. 3s. 6d. net.

Dick (Chas. Hill).
NINETEENTH CENTURY PASTORALS. Crown 8vo. 5s. net.
[*In preparation.*]

Dix (Gertrude).
THE GIRL FROM THE FARM. Crown 8vo. 3s. 6d. net. [*Second Edition.*]

Dostoievsky (F.).
POOR FOLK. Translated from the Russian by LENA MILMAN. With a Preface by GEORGE MOORE. Crown 8vo. 3s. 6d. net.

Dowie (Menie Muriel).
SOME WHIMS OF FATE. Post 8vo. 2s. 6d. net.

Duer (Caroline, and Alice).
POEMS. Fcap. 8vo. 3s. 6d. net.

Egerton (George).
KEYNOTES. Crown 8vo. 3s. 6d. net.
[*Eighth Edition.*]
DISCORDS. Crown 8vo 3s. 6d. net.
[*Fifth Edition.*]
SYMPHONIES. Crown 8vo. 6s.
[*Second Edition.*]
FANTASIAS. Crown 8vo. 3s. 6d.
THE HAZARD OF THE ILL. Crown 8vo. 6s. [*In preparation.*]

Eglinton (John).
TWO ESSAYS ON THE REMNANT. Post 8vo, wrappers. 1s. 6d. net.
[*Second Edition.*]

Farr (Florence).

THE DANCING FAUN. Crown 8vo. 3s. 6d. net.

Fea (Allan).

THE FLIGHT OF THE KING: A full, true, and particular account of the escape of His Most Sacred Majesty King Charles II. after the Battle of Worcester, with Sixteen Portraits in Photogravure and over 100 other Illustrations. Demy 8vo. 21s. net.

Field (Eugene).

THE LOVE AFFAIRS OF A BIBLIO-MANIAC. Post 8vo. 3s. 6d. net. LULLABY LAND: Songs of Childhood. Edited, with Introduction, by KENNETH GRAHAME. With 200 Illustrations by CHAS. ROBINSON. Uncut or gilt edges. Crown 8vo. 6s.

Firth (George).

THE ADVENTURES OF A MARTYR'S BIBLE. Crown 8vo. 6s.

Fleming (George).

FOR PLAIN WOMEN ONLY. Fcap. 8vo. 3s. 6d. net.

Flowerdew (Herbert).

A CELIBATE'S WIFE. Crown 8vo. 6s.

Fletcher (J. S.).

THE WONDERFUL WAPENTAKE. By "A SON OF THE SOIL." With 18 Full-page Illustrations by J. A. SYMINGTON. Crown 8vo. 5s. 6d. net. LIFE IN ARCADIA. With 20 Illustrations by PATTEN WILSON. Crown 8vo. 5s. net. GOD'S FAILURES. Crown 8vo. 3s. 6d. net. BALLADS OF REVOLT. Sq. 32mo. 2s. 6d. net. THE MAKING OF MATTHIAS. With 40 Illustrations and Decorations by LUCY KEMP-WELCH. Crown 8vo. 5s.

Florilegium Latinum.

Celebrated Passages mostly from English Poets rendered into Latin. Edited by Rev. F. ST. JOHN THACKERAY and Rev. E. D. STONE. Crown 8vo. 5s. net.

Ford (James L.).

THE LITERARY SHOP, AND OTHER TALES. Fcap. 8vo. 3s. 6d. net.

Frederic (Harold).

MARCH HARES. Crown 8vo. 3s. 6d. net. [Third Edition. MRS. ALBERT GRUNDY: OBSERVATIONS IN PHILISTIA. Fcap. 8vo. 3s. 6d. net. [Second Edition.

Fuller (H. B.).

THE PUPPET BOOTH. Twelve Plays. Crown 8vo. 4s. 6d. net.

Gale (Norman).

ORCHARD SONGS. Fcap. 8vo. 5s. net.

Garnett (Richard).

POEMS. Crown 8vo. 5s. net. DANTE, PETRARCH, CAMOENS, cxxiv Sonnets, rendered in English. Crown 8vo. 5s. net.

Geary (Sir Nevill).

A LAWYER'S WIFE. Crown 8vo. 6s. [Second Edition.

Gibson (Charles Dana).

DRAWINGS: Eighty-Five Large Cartoons. Oblong Folio. 20s. PICTURES OF PEOPLE. Eighty-Five Large Cartoons. Oblong folio. 20s. LONDON: AS SEEN BY C. D. GIBSON. Text and Illustrations. Large folio. 12 x 18 inches. 20s. THE PEOPLE OF DICKENS. Six Large Photogravures. Proof Impressions from Plates, in a Portfolio. 20s. SKETCHES AND CARTOONS. Oblong Folio. 20s.

Gilbert (Henry).

OF NECESSITY. Crown 8vo. 3s. 6d.

Gilliat-Smith (E.)

SONGS FROM PRUDENTIUS. Pott 4to. 5s. net.

Gleig (Charles)

WHEN ALL MEN STARVE. Crown 8vo. 3s. 6d. THE EDGE OF HONESTY. Crown 8vo. 6s.

Gosse (Edmund).

THE LETTERS OF THOMAS LOVELL BEDDOES. Now first edited. Pott 8vo. 5s. net.

Grahame (Kenneth).

PAGAN PAPERS. Crown 8vo. 3s. 6d. net. [Second Edition.

THE GOLDEN AGE. Crown 8vo. 3s. 6d. net. [Eighth Edition.

DREAM DAYS. Crown 8vo. 3s. 6d. net.

THE HEADSWOMAN. Sq. 16mo. 1s. net. (Bodley Booklets.)

See EUGENE FIELD'S LULLABYLAND.

Greene (G. A.).

ITALIAN LYRISTS OF TO-DAY. Translations in the original metres from about thirty-five living Italian poets, with bibliographical and biographical notes. Crown 8vo. 5s. net. [Second Edition.

Greenwood (Frederick).

IMAGINATION IN DREAMS. Crown 8vo. 5s. net.

Grimshaw (Beatrice Ethel).

BROKEN AWAY. Crown 8vo. 3s. 6d. net.

Gwynn (Stephen).

THE REPENTANCE OF A PRIVATE SECRETARY. Crown 8vo. 3s. 6d.

Hake (T. Gordon).

A SELECTION FROM HIS POEMS. Edited by Mrs. MEYNELL. With a Portrait after D. G. ROSSETTI. Crown 8vo. 5s. net.

Hansson (Laura M.).

MODERN WOMEN. An English rendering of "DAS BUCH DER FRAUEN" by HERMIONE RAMSDEN. Subjects: Sonia Kovalevsky, George Egerton, Eleanora Duse, Amalie Skram, Marie Bashkirtseff, A. Ch. Edgren Leffler. Crown 8vo. 3s. 6d. net.

WE WOMEN AND OUR AUTHORS. Translated from the German by HERMIONE RAMSDEN. Crown 8vo. 3s. 6d. net.

Hansson (Ola).

YOUNG OFEG'S DITTIES. A Translation from the Swedish. By GEORGE EGERTON. Crown 8vo. 3s. 6d. net.

Harland (Henry).

GREY ROSES. Crown 8vo. 3s. 6d. net.

COMEDIES AND ERRORS. Crown 8vo. 6s.

Hawker (Robert Stephen, of Morwenstow).

THE COMPLETE POETICAL WORKS. Crown 8vo. 5s. net.

Hay (Colonel John).

POEMS INCLUDING "THE PIKE COUNTY BALLADS" (Author's Edition), with Portrait of the Author. Crown 8vo. 4s. 6d. net.

CASTILIAN DAYS. Crown 8vo. 4s. 6d. net.

SPEECH AT THE UNVEILING OF THE BUST OF SIR WALTER SCOTT IN WESTMINSTER ABBEY. With a Drawing of the Bust. Sq. 16mo. 1s. net.

Hayes (Alfred).

THE VALE OF ARDEN AND OTHER POEMS. Fcap. 8vo. 3s. 6d. net.

Hazlitt (William).

LIBER AMORIS; OR, THE NEW PYGMALION. Edited, with an Introduction, by RICHARD LE GALLIENNE. To which is added an exact transcript of the original MS., Mrs. Hazlitt's Diary in Scotland, and letters never before published. Portrait after BEWICK, and facsimile letters. 400 Copies only. 4to, 364 pp., buckram. 21s. net.

Heinemann (William).

THE FIRST STEP; A Dramatic Moment. Small 4to. 3s. 6d. net.

SUMMER MOTHS: A Play. Sm. 4to. 3s. 6d. net.

Henniker (Florence).

IN SCARLET AND GREY. (With THE SPECTRE OF THE REAL by FLORENCE HENNIKER and THOMAS HARDY.) Crown 8vo. 3s. 6d. net. [Second Edition.

Hewlett (Maurice).
PAN AND THE YOUNG SHEPHERD :
A Pastoral. Crown 8vo. 3s. 6d.

Hickson (Mrs. Murray).
SHADOWS OF LIFE. Crown 8vo.
3s. 6d.

Hopper (Nora).
BALLADS IN PROSE. Sm. 4to. 6s.
UNDER QUICKEN BOUGHS. Crown
8vo. 5s. net.

Housman (Clemence).
THE WERE WOLF. With 6 Illustra-
tions by LAURENCE HOUSMAN.
Sq. 16mo. 3s. 6d. net.

Housman (Laurence).
GREEN ARRAS : Poems. With 6
Illustrations, Title-page, Cover
Design, and End Papers by the
Author. Crown 8vo. 5s. net.
GODS AND THEIR MAKERS. Crown
8vo, 3s. 6d. net.

Irving (Laurence).
GODEFROI AND YOLANDE : A Play.
Sm. 4to. 3s. 6d. net.

Jalland (G. H.)
THE SPORTING ADVENTURES OF
MR. POPPLE. Coloured Plates.
Oblong 4to, 14 × 10 inches. 6s.

James (W. P.)
ROMANTIC PROFESSIONS : A Volume
of Essays. Crown 8vo. 5s. net.

Johnson (Lionel).
THE ART OF THOMAS HARDY : Six
Essays. With Etched Portrait by
WM. STRANG, and Bibliography
by JOHN LANE. Crown 8vo.
5s. 6d. net. [Second Edition.

Johnson (Pauline).
WHITE WAMPUM : Poems. Crown
8vo. 5s. net.

Johnstone (C. E.).
BALLADS OF BOY AND BEAK. Sq.
32mo. 2s. net.

Kemble (E. W.)
KEMBLE'S COONS. 30 Drawings of
Coloured Children and Southern
Scenes. Oblong 4to. 6s.
A COON ALPHABET 4to. 4s. 6d.

King (K. Douglas).
THE CHILD WHO WILL NEVER GROW
OLD. Crown 8vo. 5s.

King (Maud Egerton).
ROUND ABOUT A BRIGHTON COACH
OFFICE. With over 30 Illustra-
tions by LUCY KEMP-WELCH.
Crown 8vo. 5s. net.

Lander (Harry).
WEIGHED IN THE BALANCE
Crown 8vo. 6s.

The Lark.
BOOK THE FIRST. Containing
Nos. 1 to 12.

BOOK THE SECOND. Containing
Nos. 13 to 24. With numerous
Illustrations by GELETT BURGESS
and Others. Small 4to. 25s. net.
the set. [All published.

Leather (R. K.).
VERSES. 250 copies. Fcap. 8vo.
3s. net.

Lefroy (Edward Cracroft)
POEMS. With a Memoir by W. A.
GILL, and a reprint of Mr. J. A.
SYMONDS' Critical Essay on
" Echoes from Theocritus." Cr.
8vo. Photogravure Portrait. 5s.
net.

Le Gallienne (Richard).
PROSE FANCIES. With a Portrait of
the Author by WILSON STEER.
Crown 8vo. 5s. net.
[Fourth Edition.

THE BOOK BILLS OF NARCISSUS.
An Account rendered by RICHARD
LE GALLIENNE. With a Frontis-
piece. Crown 8vo. 3s. 6d. net.
[Third Edition.

ROBERT LOUIS STEVENSON, AN
ELEGY, AND OTHER POEMS,
MAINLY PERSONAL. Crown 8vo.
4s. 6d. net.

ENGLISH POEMS. Crown 8vo.
4s. 6d. net.
[Fourth Edition, revised.

Le Gallienne (Richard)—
continued.

GEORGE MEREDITH: Some Characteristics. With a Bibliography (much enlarged) by JOHN LANE, portrait, &c. Crown 8vo. 5s. 6d. net. [Fourth Edition.

THE RELIGION OF A LITERARY MAN. Crown 8vo. 3s. 6d. net. [Fifth Thousand.

RETROSPECTIVE REVIEWS, A LITERARY LOG, 1891-1895. 2 vols. Crown 8vo. 9s. net.

PROSE FANCIES. (Second Series). Crown 8vo. 5s. net.

THE QUEST OF THE GOLDEN GIRL. Crown 8vo. 6s. [Fifth Edition.

THE ROMANCE OF ZION CHAPEL. Crown 8vo. 6s.

A VINDICATION OF EVE, AND OTHER POEMS. Crown 8vo. 4s. 6d. net. [In preparation.

See also HAZLITT, WALTON and COTTON.

Legge (A. E. J.).
MUTINEERS. Crown 8vo. 6s.

Linden (Annie).
GOLD. A Dutch Indian story. Crown 8vo. 3s. 6d. net.

Lipsett (Caldwell).
WHERE THE ATLANTIC MEETS THE LAND. Crown 8vo. 3s. 6d. net.

Locke (W. J.).
DERELICTS. Crown 8vo. 6s. [Second Edition.

IDOLS. Crown 8vo. 6s.

A STUDY IN SHADOWS. Crown 8vo. 3s. 6d.

Lowry (H. D.).
MAKE BELIEVE. Illustrated by CHARLES ROBINSON. Crown 8vo, gilt edges or uncut. 6s.

WOMEN'S TRAGEDIES. Crown 8vo. 3s. 6d. net.

THE HAPPY EXILE. With 6 Etchings by E. PHILIP PIMLOTT. Crown 8vo. 6s.

Lucas (Winifred).
UNITS: Poems. Fcap. 8vo. 3s. 6d. net.

Lynch (Hannah).
THE GREAT GALEOTO AND FOLLY OR SAINTLINESS. Two Plays, from the Spanish of JOSÉ ECHEGARAY, with an Introduction. Small 4to. 5s. 6d. net.

McChesney (Dora Greenwell).
BEATRIX INFELIX. A Summer Tragedy in Rome. Crown 8vo. 3s. 6d.

Macgregor (Barrington).
KING LONGBEARD. With over 100 Illustrations by CHARLES ROBINSON. Small 4to. 6s.

Machen (Arthur).
THE GREAT GOD PAN AND THE INMOST LIGHT. Crown 8vo. 3s. 6d. net. [Second Edition.

THE THREE IMPOSTORS. Crown 8vo. 3s. 6d. net.

Macleod (Fiona).
THE MOUNTAIN LOVERS. Crown 8vo. 3s. 6d. net.

Makower (Stanley V.).
THE MIRROR OF MUSIC. Crown 8vo. 3s. 6d. net.

CECILIA. Crown 8vo. 5s.

Mangan (James Clarence).
SELECTED POEMS. With a Biographical and Critical Preface by LOUISE IMOGEN GUINEY. Crown 8vo. 5s. net.

Mathew (Frank).
THE WOOD OF THE BRAMBLES. Crown 8vo. 6s.

A CHILD IN THE TEMPLE. Crown 8vo. 3s. 6d.

THE SPANISH WINE. Crown 8vo. 3s. 6d.

AT THE RISING OF THE MOON. Crown 8vo. 3s. 6d.

Marzials (Theo.).
THE GALLERY OF PIGEONS AND OTHER POEMS. Post 8vo. 4s. 6d. net.

Meredith (George).
THE FIRST PUBLISHED PORTRAIT OF THIS AUTHOR, engraved on the wood by W. BISCOMBE GARDNER, after the painting by G. F. WATTS. Proof copies on Japanese vellum, signed by painter and engraver. £1 1s. net.

Meynell (Mrs.).
POEMS. Fcap. 8vo. 3s. 6d. net.
[Sixth Edition.
THE RHYTHM OF LIFE AND OTHER ESSAYS. Fcap. 8vo. 3s. 6d. net.
[Sixth Edition.
THE COLOUR OF LIFE AND OTHER ESSAYS. Fcap. 8vo. 3s. 6d. net. [Fifth Edition.
THE CHILDREN. Fcap. 8vo. 3s. 6d. net. [Second Edition.
THE SPIRIT OF PLACE AND OTHER ESSAYS. Fcap. 8vo. 3s. 6d. net.

Miall (A. Bernard).
POEMS. Crown 8vo. 5s. net.

Miller (Joaquin).
THE BUILDING OF THE CITY BEAUTIFUL. Fcap. 8vo. With a Decorated Cover. 5s. net.

Milman (Helen).
IN THE GARDEN OF PEACE. With 24 Illustrations by EDMUND H. NEW. Crown 8vo. 5s. net.
[Second Edition.

Money-Coutts (F. B.).
POEMS. Crown 8vo. 3s. 6d. net.
THE REVELATION OF ST. LOVE THE DIVINE. Sq. 16mo. 3s. 6d. net.
THE ALHAMBRA AND OTHER POEMS. Crown 8vo. 3s. 6d. net.

Monkhouse (Allan).
BOOKS AND PLAYS: A Volume of Essays on Meredith, Borrow, Ibsen, and others. Crown 8vo. 5s. net.
A DELIVERANCE. Crown 8vo. 3s. 6d.

Nesbit (E.).
A POMANDER OF VERSE. Crown 8vo. 5s. net.
IN HOMESPUN. Crown 8vo. 3s. 6d. net.

Nettleship (J. T.).
ROBERT BROWNING: Essays and Thoughts. Portrait. Crown 8vo. 5s. 6d. net. [Third Edition.

Nicholson (Claud).
UGLY IDOL. Crown 8vo. 3s. 6d. net.

Noble (Jas. Ashcroft).
THE SONNET IN ENGLAND AND OTHER ESSAYS. Crown 8vo. 5s. net.

Oppenheim (M.).
A HISTORY OF THE ADMINISTRATION OF THE ROYAL NAVY, and of Merchant Shipping in relation to the Navy from MDIX to MDCLX, with an introduction treating of the earlier period. With Illustrations. Demy 8vo. 15s. net.

Orred (Meta).
GLAMOUR. Crown 8vo. 6s.

O'Shaughnessy (Arthur).
HIS LIFE AND HIS WORK. With Selections from his Poems. By LOUISE CHANDLER MOULTON. Portrait and Cover Design. Fcap. 8vo. 5s. net.

Oxford Characters.
A series of lithographed portraits by WILL ROTHENSTEIN, with text by F. YORK POWELL and others. 200 copies only, folio. £3 3s. net.

Pain (Barry).
THE TOMPKINS VERSES. Edited by BARRY PAIN, with an introduction. Crown 8vo. 3s. 6d.

Pennell (Elizabeth Robins).
THE FEASTS OF AUTOLYCUS: THE DIARY OF A GREEDY WOMAN. Fcap. 8vo. 3s. 6d. net.

Peters (Wm. Theodore).
POSIES OUT OF RINGS. Sq. 16mo. 2s. 6d. net.

Phillips (Stephen)
POEMS. With which is incorporated "CHRIST IN HADES." Crown 8vo. 4s. 6d. net.
[*Fifth Edition.*

Pinkerton (T. A.).
SUN BEETLES. Crown 8vo. 3s. 6d.

Plarr (Victor).
IN THE DORIAN MOOD: Poems Crown 8vo. 5s. net.

Posters in Miniature: over 250 reproductions of French, English and American Posters, with Introduction by EDWARD PENFIELD. Large crown 8vo. 5s. net.

Price (A. T. G.).
SIMPLICITY. Sq. 16mo. 2s. net.

Radford (Dollie).
SONGS AND OTHER VERSES. Fcap. 8vo. 4s. 6d. net.

Rands (W. B).
LILLIPUT LYRICS. Edited by R. BRIMLEY JOHNSON. With 140 Illustrations by CHARLES ROBINSON. Crown 8vo. 6s.

Richardson (E.).
SUN, MOON, AND STARS: PICTURES AND VERSES FOR CHILDREN. Demy 12mo. 2s. 6d.

Risley (R. V.).
THE SENTIMENTAL VIKINGS. Post 8vo. 2s. 6d. net.

Rhys (Ernest).
A LONDON ROSE AND OTHER RHYMES. Crown 8vo. 5s. net.

Robertson (John M.).
NEW ESSAYS TOWARDS A CRITICAL METHOD. Crown 8vo. 6s. net.

Russell (T. Baron).
A GUARDIAN OF THE POOR. Crown 8vo. 3s. 6d.

St. Cyres (Lord).
THE LITTLE FLOWERS OF ST. FRANCIS: A new rendering into English of the Fioretti di San Francesco. Crown 8vo. 5s. net
[*In preparation.*

Seaman (Owen).
THE BATTLE OF THE BAYS. Fcap. 8vo. 3s. 6d. net. [*Fourth Edition.*
HORACE AT CAMBRIDGE. Crown 8vo. 3s. 6d. net.

Sedgwick (Jane Minot).
SONGS FROM THE GREEK. Fcap. 8vo. 3s. 6d. net.

Setoun (Gabriel).
THE CHILD WORLD: Poems. With over 200 Illustrations by CHARLES ROBINSON. Crown 8vo, gilt edges or uncut. 6s.

Shakespeare's Sonnets.
Illustrated by H. OSPOVAT. Sq. 16mo. 3s. 6d. net.

Sharp (Evelyn).
WYMPS: Fairy Tales. With 8 Coloured Illustrations by Mrs. PERCY DEARMER. Small 4to, decorated cover. 6s. [*Second Edition.*
Also a New Edition, paper boards. 3s. 6d.
AT THE RELTON ARMS. Crown 8vo. 3s. 6d. net.
THE MAKING OF A PRIG. Crown 8vo. 6s.
ALL THE WAY TO FAIRY LAND. With 8 Coloured Illustrations by Mrs. PERCY DEARMER. Small 4to, decorated cover. 6s.
[*Second Edition.*

Shelley (Percy Bysshe and Elizabeth).
ORIGINAL POETRY. By VICTOR and CAZIRE. A reprint *verbatim et literatim* from the unique copy of the First Edition. Edited by Dr. GARNETT. Demy 8vo. 5s. net.

Shiel (M. P.).
PRINCE ZALESKI. Crown 8vo. 3s. 6d. net.
SHAPES IN THE FIRE. Crown 8vo. 3s. 6d. net.

Shore (Louisa).
POEMS. With an appreciation by FREDERIC HARRISON and a Portrait. Fcap. 8vo. 5s. net.

Shorter (Mrs. Clement) (Dora Sigerson).
THE FAIRY CHANGELING, AND OTHER POEMS. Crown 8vo. 3s. 6d. net.

Skram (Amalie).

PROFESSOR HIERONIMUS. Translated from the Danish by ALICE STRONACH and G. B. JACOBI. Crown 8vo. 6s.

Smith (John).

PLATONIC AFFECTIONS. Crown 8vo. 3s. 6d. net.

Stacpoole (H. de Vere).

PIERROT. Sq. 16mo. 2s. net.
DEATH, THE KNIGHT, AND THE LADY Crown 8vo. 3s. 6d.
PIERRETTE, HER BOOK. With 20 Illustrations by CHARLES ROBINSON. Crown 8vo. 6s.

Stevenson (Robert Louis).

PRINCE OTTO. A Rendering in French by EGERTON CASTLE. Crown 8vo. 7s. 6d. net.
A CHILD'S GARDEN OF VERSES. With over 150 Illustrations by CHARLES ROBINSON. Crown 8vo. 5s. net.   [Fifth Edition.

Stimson (F. J.).

KING NOANETT. A Romance of Devonshire Settlers in New England. With 12 Illustrations by HENRY SANDHAM. Crown 8vo. 6s.

Stoddart (Thos. Tod).

THE DEATH WAKE. With an Introduction by ANDREW LANG. Fcap. 8vo. 5s. net.

Street (G. S.).

EPISODES. Post 8vo. 3s. net.
MINIATURES AND MOODS. Fcap. 8vo. 3s. net.
QUALES EGO: A FEW REMARKS, IN PARTICULAR AND AT LARGE. Fcap. 8vo. 3s. 6d. net.
THE AUTOBIOGRAPHY OF A BOY. Fcap. 8vo. 3s. 6d. net.   [Sixth Edition.
THE WISE AND THE WAYWARD. Crown 8vo. 6s.
SOME NOTES OF A STRUGGLING GENIUS. Sq. 16mo, wrapper. 2s. net.

Sudermann (H.).

REGINA: OR, THE SINS OF THE FATHERS. A Translation of DER KATZENSTEG. By BEATRICE MARSHALL. Crown 8vo. 6s.   [Second Edition.

Swettenham (Sir F. A.)

MALAY SKETCHES. Crown 8vo. 6s.   [Second Edition.
UNADDRESSED LETTERS. Crown 8vo. 6s.

Syrett (Netta).

NOBODY'S FAULT. Crown 8vo. 3s. 6d. net.   [Second Edition.
THE TREE OF LIFE. Crown 8vo. 6s.   [Second Edition.

Tabb (John B.).

POEMS. Sq. 32mo. 4s. 6d. net.
LYRICS. Sq. 32mo. 4s. 6d. net.

Taylor (Una),

NETS FOR THE WIND. Crown 8vo. 3s. 6d. net.

Temper (Charles).

THE ROMANCE OF A RITUALIST. Crown 8vo. 6s.

Tennyson (Frederick).

POEMS OF THE DAY AND YEAR. Crown 8vo. 5s. net.

Thimm (Carl A.).

A COMPLETE BIBLIOGRAPHY OF FENCING AND DUELLING, AS PRACTISED BY ALL EUROPEAN NATIONS FROM THE MIDDLE AGES TO THE PRESENT DAY. With a Classified Index, arranged Chronologically according to Languages. Illustrated with numerous Portraits of Ancient and Modern Masters of the Art. Title-pages and Frontispieces of some of the earliest works. Portrait of the Author by WILSON STEER. 4to. 21s. net.

Thompson (Francis)

POEMS. With Frontispiece by LAURENCE HOUSMAN. Pott 4to. 5s. net.   [Fourth Edition.
SISTER-SONGS: An Offering to Two Sisters. With Frontispiece by LAURENCE HOUSMAN. Pott 4to. 5s. net.

Thoreau (Henry David).
 POEMS OF NATURE. Selected and edited by HENRY S. SALT and FRANK B. SANBORN. Fcap. 8vo. 4s. 6d. net.

Traill (H. D.).
 THE BARBAROUS BRITISHERS: A Tip-top Novel. Crown 8vo, wrapper. 1s. net.
 FROM CAIRO TO THE SOUDAN FRONTIER. Crown 8vo. 5s. net.

Tynan Hinkson (Katharine).
 CUCKOO SONGS. Fcap. 8vo. 5s. net.
 MIRACLE PLAYS. OUR LORD'S COMING AND CHILDHOOD. With 6 Illustrations by PATTEN WILSON. Fcap. 8vo. 4s. 6d. net.

Verhaeren (Emile).
 POEMS. Selected and Rendered into English by ALMA STRETTELL. Crown 8vo. 5s. net.

Walton and Cotton.
 THE COMPLEAT ANGLER. Edited by RICHARD LE GALLIENNE. With over 250 Illustrations by EDMUND H. NEW. Fcap. 4to, decorated cover. 15s. net.
 Also to be had in thirteen 1s. parts.

Warden (Gertrude).
 THE SENTIMENTAL SEX. Crown 8vo. 3s. 6d. net.

Watson (H. B. Marriott).
 AT THE FIRST CORNER AND OTHER STORIES. Crown 8vo. 3s. 6d. net.
 GALLOPING DICK. Crown 8vo. 6s.
 THE HEART OF MIRANDA. Crown 8vo. 6s.

Watson (Rosamund Marriott).
 VESPERTILIA AND OTHER POEMS. Fcap. 8vo. 4s. 6d. net.
 A SUMMER NIGHT AND OTHER POEMS. New Edition. Fcap. 8vo. 3s. net.

Watson (William).
 THE COLLECTED POEMS. Crown 8vo. With Portrait. 7s. 6d. net.
 Also a Large Paper Edition on Handmade paper, limited to 75 Copies. 21s. net.

Watson (William)—continued
 THE PRINCE'S QUEST AND OTHER POEMS. Fcap. 8vo. 4s. 6d. net.
  [Third Edition.
 POEMS. Fcap. 8vo. 3s. 6d. net.
  [Fifth Edition.
 LACHRYMAE MUSARUM. Fcap. 8vo, 3s. 6d. net. [Fourth Edition.

 THE ELOPING ANGELS: A Caprice. Square 16mo. 3s. 6d. net.
  [Second Edition.

 ODES AND OTHER POEMS. Fcap. 8vo. 4s. 6d. net.
  [Fifth Edition.

 THE FATHER OF THE FOREST AND OTHER POEMS. With Photogravure Portrait of the Author. Fcap. 8vo. 3s. 6d. net.
  [Fifth Edition.

 THE PURPLE EAST: A Series of Sonnets on England's Desertion of Armenia. With a Frontispiece after G. F. WATTS, R.A. Fcap. 8vo, wrappers. 1s. net.
  [Third Edition.

 THE YEAR OF SHAME. With an Introduction by the BISHOP OF HEREFORD. Fcap. 8vo. 3s. 6d. net. [Second Edition.

 THE HOPE OF THE WORLD, AND OTHER POEMS. Fcap. 8vo. 3s. 6d. net. [Third Edition.

 EXCURSIONS IN CRITICISM: being some Prose Recreations of a Rhymer. Crown 8vo. 5s. net.
  [Second Edition.

Watt (Francis).
 THE LAW'S LUMBER ROOM. Fcap. 8vo. 3s. 6d. net.
  [Second Edition.

 THE LAW'S LUMBER ROOM. Second Series. Fcap. 8vo. 4s. 6d. net.

Watts-Dunton (Theodore).
 JUBILEE GREETING AT SPITHEAD TO THE MEN OF GREATER BRITAIN. Crown 8vo. 1s. net.

 THE COMING OF LOVE AND OTHER POEMS. Crown 8vo. 5s. net.
  [Second Edition.

Wells (H. G.)

SELECT CONVERSATIONS WITH AN UNCLE, NOW EXTINCT. Fcap. 8vo. 3s. 6d. net.

Wenzell (A. B.)

IN VANITY FAIR. 70 Drawings. Oblong folio. 20s.

Wharton (H. T.)

SAPPHO. Memoir, Text, Selected Renderings, and a Literal Translation by HENRY THORNTON WHARTON. With 3 Illustrations in Photogravure, and a Cover designed by AUBREY BEARDSLEY. With a Memoir of Mr. Wharton. Fcap. 8vo. 6s. net.

[Fourth Edition.

White (Gilbert).

THE NATURAL HISTORY OF SELBORNE. Edited by GRANT ALLEN. With nearly 200 Illustrations by EDMUND H. NEW. Fcap. 4to., buckram. 15s. net. *Also an Edition printed on hand-made paper. Limited to 100 copies for England and America. Fcap. 4to. 42s. net.*

Wotton (Mabel E.).

DAY BOOKS. Crown 8vo. 3s. 6d. net.

Xenopoulos (Gregory).

THE STEPMOTHER: A TALE OF MODERN ATHENS. Translated by MRS. EDMONDS. Crown 8vo. 2s. 6d. net.

Zola (Emile).

FOUR LETTERS TO FRANCE—THE DREYFUS AFFAIR. Fcap. 8vo, wrapper. 1s. net.

THE YELLOW BOOK

An Illustrated Quarterly.

Pott 4to. 5s. net.

I. April 1894, 272 pp., 15 Illustrations. [*Out of print.*

II. July 1894, 364 pp., 23 Illustrations.

III. October 1894, 280 pp., 15 Illustrations.

IV. January 1895, 285 pp., 16 Illustrations.

V. April 1895, 317 pp., 14 Illustrations.

VI. July 1895, 335 pp., 16 Illustrations.

VII. October 1895, 320 pp., 20 Illustrations.

VIII. January 1896, 406 pp., 26 Illustrations.

IX. April 1896, 256 pp., 17 Illustrations.

X. July 1896, 340 pp., 13 Illustrations.

XI. October 1896, 342 pp., 12 Illustrations.

XII. January 1897, 350 pp., 14 Illustrations.

XIII. April 1897, 316 pp., 18 Illustrations.

www.ingramcontent.com/pod-product-compliance
Lightning Source LLC
Chambersburg PA
CBHW060528030726
47498CB00004B/1118